CHILDREN
OF THE
SPIDER

BY IMAM BAKSH

Blouse and Skirt Books, Kingston.

© Imam Baksh 2016
Children of the Spider

First published in Kingston by Blouse & Skirt Books, 2016

Blouse & Skirt Books is an imprint of Blue Moon Publishing

A CIP catalogue record of this book is available from the National Library of Jamaica

ISBN 978-976-8267-01-6

Cover Image by Dandre Foster

Cover Design by Nucleus Creative

Maps by Imam Baksh

Blue Moon Publishing
PO Box 5464
Liguanea PO
Kingston 6
Jamaica, W.I.

www.blumoonbooks.com

Thanks are due to CODE, The Burt Award for Caribbean Literature and the Bocas Literary Festival

For my parents, who started me on books.

Thanks to Maraiyah and Aadil for their advice and to my editor, Tanya Batson-Savage, for insisting I make it even better.

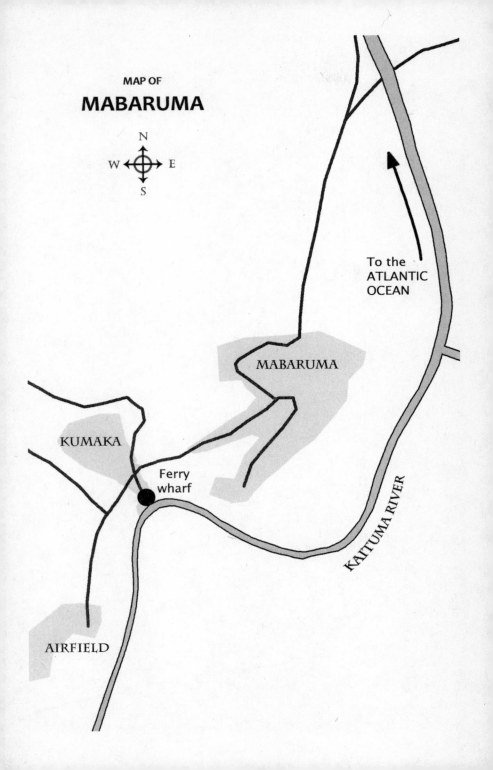

MAP OF
GEORGETOWN

ATLANTIC OCEAN

DEMERARA RIVER

N
W ⊕ E
S

1 - STABROEK MARKET
2 - BOTANICAL GARDENS
3 - PRASHAD NAGAR
4 - SOPHIA
5 - PRESIDENT'S RESIDENCE
6 - HILADORA STEEL
7 - ABANDONED FACTORY
8 - RADIO STATION
9 - ARMY HQ
10 - WATER PLANT
11 - OGLE AIRSTRIP

Church St

Regent St

Sherrif St

Mandela Ave

CHILDREN
OF THE
SPIDER

PROLOGUE

In the land of the Spider gods, a girl counted the stars and waited.

The hillside where she crouched was exposed to the eyes of the enemy, with just a few mossy and pungent boulders for cover, but their heads bent in prayer around the fountain below, the men never looked up from under their hoods. They lit flambeaus and put them out again in an order only they understood. Seven of the Brothers wore black robes. The eighth wore red and carried a spear.

In the land of her mother's grave and her father's memory, a girl waited.

When had she last eaten? There were candyberries in the offering plates next to the fires. Her father had told her about real candy once when she was a much smaller girl. Her little self had marvelled at the idea of candy that was actually sweet. The name 'candyberry' started as a joke, her father had explained. Tonight, the girl on the hillside was still not fully grown, but she knew that the time for growing up was over.

In the land of cloudfire, snakeskin houses and hardwater roads, a girl waited.

The stars of the Fisherman had frozen in place, glowing brighter as the moon rose into the centre of the constellation. It was almost time. The girl hoped Jalana and the other rocksliders were hiding in the right place. She hoped that they would keep their word. She wondered if she could keep hers.

The man in the red robe lifted his spear to the sky and the water in the fountain exploded with golden light. The girl ran down the hill, bare feet on rocky ground. Which of them would see her first?

The biggest one. Why did it have to be the biggest one?

The man's head came up, then his robed hand, pointing as he screeched the alarm. The girl was not even halfway there and she had been discovered. Should she pull her knife and fight?

But the rest of the Brothers were distracted, watching the far side of the fountain. Rocks were flying at them and they scattered under the attack. On the far hills the girl could make out the glowing, blobby forms of the rocksliders. They sucked up rocks from below with their feeding maws and spat them at the robed men through the tops of their bodies.

The fountain was unguarded by the time the girl got there. A few late-arriving rocks smashed behind her. The mark of Arrak was inscribed on the tray holding the candyberries. She grabbed a handful and stuffed her mouth with the bitter fruit, letting them slide down her gullet. The fountain bubbled. It was more water than she had ever seen in her life. Was it even safe to jump into it?

Too late to wonder now. Jalana's people were already fleeing. The skin that held their sloshy bodies together was vulnerable to the Brothers' arrows and they could not risk staying in the open long. The girl jumped into the water and sank. At least it didn't matter that she couldn't swim. Her lungs burned as she searched out the bottom descending towards the light which grew brighter and clearer as she went deeper. For weeks she had practiced holding her breath in preparation for this, but in the end it was not enough. Water invaded her nose, burning and making her eyes hurt. The world seemed to twist around her and she broke through the other side into sunlight. There was no neat fountain at this end of the portal just a shallow, swampy pond. She gasped as she crawled to the shore, then curled up within the roots of an endlessly tall tree.

It was daylight. She could tell by the angle of the shadows, but the new place was dark. The treetops hung like low clouds. From the stories she had heard, Mayali had expected to feel a thrill at the sight of so many leaves, but this world of endless green seemed ominous. It was like life was out of control here. How did people survive? Well, she would learn just as she had learned to climb down rock faces to steal from the Brothers or learned to tunnel for snakeskins.

The pond bubbled behind her. Were they following her to this new world? It seemed unlikely. The fanatics on the other side were taught that women corrupted water and now that the girl had used the fountain, they probably believed it to be diseased. It was her bleeding time of the month too. She smiled. She hoped they could taste it when they drank from their stupid fountain. Of course, it was more likely that they would fill the thing with dirt rather than touch it again.

She would never return home. This new place was the rest of her life now. Somewhere, in this strange, over-green world, was her father. She would rest until dark then sneak out and begin her search and soon she would need to find help for those she had left at home.

In the land of Guyana, the land of many waters, a girl drew her knife and waited.

CHAPTER 1

Joseph and the Radio Police

The teenaged boy with the red backpack travelled up the hill on foot looking neither left nor right when he passed anyone, his eyes on the pale dirt ahead. He itched to check his phone messages, but Joseph kept careful watch for anything that might trip him instead. He knew the road well but did not want to risk an accident that could damage anything in the bag.

Joseph was at least satisfied that he had received the most important message before leaving home: *Lady Northcote* was running late, as usual, but the ship would be in Mabaruma before dark and there were no inspectors on board the ship today. He could see her already in his mind, that odd combination of upright, streamlined prow and blocky body, struggling upriver on half an engine while still looking dignified.

The church sat at the top of the rise framed by breadfruit trees. Standing above everything was the wooden bell tower with the large white cross on top. From the hilltop, Joseph could see the curving river, scattered housetops and, of course, trees. Mabaruma was plumb in the middle of the jungle, and waves of dark green stretched to every horizon.

Father Garcia was in the front garden, kneeling by some large purple flowers. He waved, speaking words Joseph could not hear, but which he knew to be 'Good Morning'.

Joseph signed, "Good Morning," in the way the priest had taught him and smiled.

"You seem happy," the man signed back.

Joseph made the sign for the billowing smoke of the steamer.

"Oh, it's here?"

The boy nodded with a smile then went inside. He caught sight of the new kitchen girl down the corridor by the stove. Whatever she was cooking smelled over-spiced and maybe burnt. The girl herself looked determined as she poked at the pot with a wooden spoon. Like Joseph and most people in the area, she was Amerindian. Her body was slim and she kept her hair straight and short, creating an unusual mop-headed style. Joseph guessed she was about fifteen, a year or so younger than him. The girl wore a long skirt over her jeans since Father Garcia thought that jeans were unfeminine, and a short-sleeved man's shirt, that was large for her.

Joseph turned toward the tower stairs. The new girl was quiet and had never teased Joseph about being a deaf-mute, but he still kept his distance. He was not good at dealing with people, at least not face-to-face, and this girl wore a fierce look when she thought no one was around, except when Joseph would sometimes see her in the top of a breadfruit tree, looking out at the river. Then the expression on her face was soft.

Father Garcia had arranged for the girl to help him in the kitchen after meeting her at Aunty Janice's foster home a few months before. She had been using a pencil to draw rather than write and Father Garcia had decided that she had talent. Nowadays, she spent some time inexpertly doing chores and then drawing, painting or even experimenting with artistic wood burning outside. Joseph had observed all this from a safe distance. He still could not say what the girl's name was.

He came to the eastern end of the building. After two flights of stairs it was a quick trip up a ladder to the platform under the bell. Joseph drew the ladder up after himself and sat flat on the unpolished wooden floor, setting his shoes aside. He took a laptop from his bag and turned it on. He laid his cell phone on the ground, making sure to switch the SIM card with one he kept in a hidden fold at the bottom of his backpack.

As the computer flashed to life, Joseph took a yellow electrical multi-meter from the bag and climbed higher into the tower, using the crossbeams. He followed a thin wire painted the same dirty cream as the rest of the tower's interior. He stopped near the top, pulling his long hair back behind his ear so he could see. Sometimes he would inspect the antenna hidden at the top of the cross outside, forty feet above the ground, but only when it was dark. Today he only checked the car battery he had set in a small space where it could not be seen from the floor. The meter told him the battery was at full power.

Joseph dropped down next to the computer, landing softly on his bare feet. He pulled a radio from his backpack and set it down with him, so he could see the big digital display in the front. It showed a straight line of silence. But that was about to change.

He sat cross-legged before the computer and clicked the icon for 'Natural Speech.' He started four other programs all sharing the screen. The radio broadcast signal began, sending static that showed up on the radio's display as scrunched lines with no order. He typed his greeting and sent it. The radio display showed the voice coming through as peaks and valleys and Joseph could tell the sound was clear. The voice he used was a mix of mechanical male speech with an American accent.

Mabaruma, get your ears out. This is Porknocker Paul starting your day off right with great news on Mabaruma Radio: The great ship is here! All you market stall people down at the river, get yourselves ready. As for the rest of my Mabaruma brothers and sisters, good morning to you.

Joseph was busy across the computer screen, monitoring the

power of the transmission through the antenna, maintaining the sound quality, making the speech sound as natural as possible from the text and queuing up his main attraction.

For all you people who started the day slow, here's some soca to get you moving. Don't be shy; let them hips fly.

Once the music started, Joseph relaxed. Faking the voice was the biggest strain. It was time to have fun. There were already twenty text messages on his phone. He picked one and typed a reply into the computer while the music played. He hit Enter when the song ended.

That was Eddy Grant making your morning a little hotter here on Mabaruma Radio. Don't forget you can text in to our show on 327-4222. We've already got a message here from Sleepy. Sleepy says, 'Porknocker Paul, I just get back from three weeks in the bush, working hard-hard and me girl don't want let me rest. All she want is romance and I can't take it no more. Three times a night she bothering me. Help.'

Well, Sleepy, I decided a man like you needs a woman's advice, so I handed it over to Lisa Love, our love doctor, to sort you out.

Here, Joseph switched settings. He not only changed the voice to a female with a British accent, but he slowed it down.

Sleepy, this is Lisa Love and I'm telling you to wake up. That woman waited three weeks for you to come home. The least you can do is make it worth her time. It's not like Mabaruma is short of men, you know. If you don't do things right when you're home, you might come back after the next three weeks and find you don't have anyone asking you for romance.

~ ~ ~ : : ~ : ~ : : ~ ~ ~

And so the morning went. Joseph played music and dropped tidbits of gossip and 'shout-outs' to different people. He used a dozen different voices from his speech program for different segments, each one given a different name and personality. His was an unlicensed and hidden operation so he had no advertisers, but he gave ads for the local businesses anyway, talking about items he had seen in there. Even Mr. de Santos, who was scornful of Joseph when the boy went into his restaurant, got a good mention for his food and his waitresses.

Mabaruma was the seat of the local government and had its own airstrip, army outpost, police outpost, and shipping wharves. There was even a secondary school that Joseph had never attended. The town was booming since it was the first step to the mining sites in the area.

Jook-Jook Man up the river says he's been seeing strange people around the place. Well, Jook-Jook, all I've got to say to that is strange people come through Mabaruma every day. People want the gold and we've got the gold. But wait – You don't suppose it might be Venezuelan spies? They might be scouting the place for an invasion you know.

Well, we can't worry about that. It's not like the army could do anything about it. Lieutenant Dasrath and his men are more interested in the rum down at Shelly's Bar than training to fight anybody. I wonder if the lieutenant knows that the Venezuelans would take his rum too? I bet he would fight then!

Joseph couldn't help teasing the soldiers. They were the ones who accompanied the inspectors when they visited Mabaruma, trooping around with their heavy equipment, trying to calculate where the illegal Radio Mabaruma signal was coming from.

Father Garcia had first encouraged and then helped Joseph with his radio project. They had pieced it together out of scraps of mining camp radios, augmenting it with home-brewed gadgetry. While it could be heard around the town, it was still a weak signal.

But in the past year, the broadcasts had become too popular, enhanced by the mystery of the multiple voices, and the broadcasting regulators had started visiting. Joseph refused to broadcast when they were around, alerted to their presence by the ground crew at the airport or the sailors on the ferry, all dedicated listeners of his show. Today, Joseph had gotten the all-clear to broadcast.

I'm just teasing about the rum, Lieutenant Dasrath. Here's some music, dedicated to the brave men and women of the Guyana Army. Remember, every little thing is gonna be all right.

A few minutes later, near the end of the Bob Marley song, a shadow from below startled Joseph causing him to knock over the radio with his foot. He saw nothing when he leaned over the side of his platform, but he dropped over the edge, almost like he was falling, except he landed upright with knees bent. Nothing down the corridor. He walked down the passageway until he could see the kitchen. The girl was in there at the counter chopping something. She looked up and scowled at him. Joseph realized he looked like he was spying and backed out of sight then rushed back to the computer. The music had ended by the time he got there and the radio had been broadcasting just a hiss.

Radio Mabaruma apologizes for that short break in transmission which was caused by technical difficulties. We resume now with the music of Eddie Neblett. But first, let's not forget that it's Donna Sankar's birthday today. This song's for her, from a secret admirer.

There was no secret admirer. But Donna's boyfriend had just left her and she could use a smile.

Joseph never used Creole. People had trouble understanding it with the accents the computer program provided. Besides, he needed to practice his English. The priest had told Joseph he could get a job operating equipment at a real radio station if he kept learning. But Joseph knew the computer voice technology was improving. He could be an on-air presenter, he was sure of it.

A shadow moved again. It had to be the girl. Joseph crept to the side on his knees and looked down.

A man in a red, hooded robe was at the far wall. The man inspected the wall with his two hands while staring at it. The eight fingers protruding from under the sleeves were hairy, almost furry, and they lifted one at a time, high above the surface, before coming down with the fingertips against the wall. The fingers moved almost like they were crawling on their own, pulling the hands up inch by inch.

The man's fingers paused, and he held still as if listening. He glanced over at Joseph who glimpsed a flash from where the man's eyes should be under the hood. The room blinked. Instead of a robed man, there was a man in a brown, long-sleeved shirt, khaki pants and leather shoes. And instead of searching the wall, the man was standing on the floor, like a normal person, looking up at Joseph with human eyes and carefully parted hair. The man spoke,

"Are you in compliance with the law?"

For the first time he could remember, Joseph heard words. But not with his ears. These words went directly into his thoughts, and they hurt. They felt like talons clawing at his brain.

Joseph gasped and lay flat to avoid falling over the edge. This man must be a radio regulator. They had found him. Joseph peered at the man again. A laminated blue badge with an electrical symbol hung around his neck and the tops of two pens peeked out of his shirt pocket.

Joseph's panic at having his pirate station busted gave way to a tide of even greater panic at what was happening to him. Why could he hear this man in his head and why did it hurt? Did hearing make people sick?

The man below was looking at him. His expression remained blank but his head was slightly tilted to the side. He spoke again, *"I am Mr. Hakk. We demand that you let us inspect—"*

The question was cut off as something down the corridor made the man turn. Joseph heard nothing, telling him that his ears had not suddenly started working. So why was he hearing this man in his head? The man briefly appeared to be wearing his robes again and then he was back in regular clothes, running down the corridor.

Without the pain of the words in his mind, Joseph's sense of balance returned. He clambered down from the ledge and ran after the inspector, worried about what the man was going to do to his radio station.

The girl was fleeing down the corridor with the inspector behind her. She ran through the doors into the main hall of the church. Joseph was faster than the man and passed through the doorway right behind him. The man cornered the girl near the pulpit, under the last intact stained glass window of the building. They were speaking aloud and Joseph could hear both of them in his head.

"Come closer and I will kill you. I'll kill you with my teeth if I have to!" the girl said, holding a hand behind her back.

The man was not listening. *"Your duty is to return, my sister. Return willingly and it will be painless,"* he kept repeating.

Joseph grabbed his head at the pain of the words in his mind.

"Stop! Stop! Both of you stop talking!"

They whirled to look at Joseph and he realized they had heard his thoughts. Light spilled into the room as Father Garcia ran in through the main doors, shouting words that did not register in Joseph's mind, mud splattering off his boots onto the carpeted aisle.

The inspector walked towards the priest. *"Sir, is this institution in compliance with the law?"*

Father Garcia's mouth worked and his expression changed from puzzled to fearful. To Joseph the man still wore a Radio Inspector's badge, but he could tell Father Garcia was seeing something else there, something that frightened him. Maybe it was an angel. Maybe it was some kind of church police.

Two more inspectors ran into the building from the side door. Their brown and grey clothes shifted in Joseph's vision to give him a glimpse of black robes, then the illusion returned. Father Garcia was yelling at the men.

"Obey. Do not resist. Comply," the men chanted.

The girl sped past Joseph without a word. The three inspectors turned to chase, but Father Garcia jumped in their way stopping two of them. As the one in the red robe, Hakk, ran toward him, Joseph realized that whatever was happening was beyond reality, beyond his hope of understanding. And he wanted to be somewhere else. He staggered backward, turned and fled after the girl.

CHAPTER 2
Breaking-and-Exiting

Mayali ran down the hill not caring where she went, just hoping that if she ran fast enough she could stay ahead of the Brothers long enough to – to what? She had waited too long to leave this place. She had known they would be looking for her, but Mayali had needed to learn the language and gather money and make a plan and - and the most important thing had been neglected – staying out of reach.

"Wait!"

It was the deaf boy, who never spoke, running behind her. Somehow he could use the Spider's Touch. Mayali kept running. The boy's trick with words was not important.

"You're going the wrong way," the boy said.

Now she slowed, looking over her shoulder at the running boy and the acolyte still coming after them about a hundred feet behind. *"What do you mean th—"*

"If we take the side track we can get to the army outpost faster."

"The army can't help us," she told him.

"Just turn left!"

And she did, realizing that it was better than wild running. It took another ten minutes, but Mayali felt relief as they ran to the gate of the army building. Its faded, sagging white walls with their green trim seemed like the most solid thing she'd ever seen. People were everywhere on the street outside and she realized that the lone acolyte would not attempt to catch her here. Not now at any rate.

Hands grabbed Mayali's shoulder from behind and she knocked them away, turning around.

"Hey! Relax!" said the boy, rubbing his elbow.

Mayali looked past him. No sign of the acolyte on the street or in the surrounding trees.

"You have to go inside," Joseph said. *"You have to tell them what happened."*

"They won't believe me."

"Well, just tell them someone tried to rob the church. They'll send people to check."

It took fifteen minutes for the guards to decide their report was serious. The sergeant on duty sent a corporal to fetch Lieutenant Dasrath from Shelly's Bar and also inform the police. After she left, eight soldiers piled into a pickup truck and sped off towards the church.

~ ~ ~ :: ~ : ~ :: ~ ~ ~

Mayali and Joseph were placed in someone's office and told to stay there until it was safe.

"Who are you?" Joseph asked when they were alone. He was pacing at the window, peering through the wooden bars crudely nailed across it for security.

"My name is Mayali," she responded without speaking aloud, so no one could eavesdrop. She sat on a bench in the far corner, watching the door.

"I don't care about your name," said Joseph. *"I mean how is it you can get into my head? That's not natural. That's not right."*

"I don't know. No one else can hear me around here. Usually, the messages pass underneath the voice without people noticing. Maybe you're from the same place as me and never knew—"

"No!" Joseph's eyes were angry. *"I'm not any kind of – whatever you are. I'm normal. I'm Godly and I—"* Fear took over his face as a new possibility occurred to him. *"Are you a demon? You don't look—"*

"I'm not a demon."

"That's what a demon would say. God will protect me against—"

She grabbed the front of his shirt and pulled him close, her face only inches away from his. "Listen," she said, "if I was a demon, I would just kill you now and shut you up, right?"

He considered it and nodded slightly.

"Good," she said, letting him go. "Now stop talking nonsense."

He backed up sullenly to a corner, smoothing out his shirt.

Mayali did not want to keep arguing, so she changed the subject. "Do we have to stay here? We told them to go to the church. We should leave before any Brothers find us."

"We can't leave." He was back to being angry. "The army told us to stay here. The army. You understand that? They have armies where you're from?"

"Yes," said Mayali, looking him in the eye. "The people who just tried to kill us. And we should be gone before they come back."

At first, Mayali hoped the look of realization on the boy's face was him understanding that they were not safe. But he looked at her with scorn and said, "So, you're a criminal?"

She rolled her eyes at him and watched the door again, trying to listen for what was happening. Out of the corner of her eye, she saw Joseph edging closer to the exit. Even if the boy could not speak, he could write. But what could he tell them about her? The truth? Would they believe him?

She smiled to herself.

"You want to know who I am?"

"Yes."

"I came to your land through a passage from another world."

Joseph was watching her as if she were insane. She understood why. The people here knew nothing about her world, but she was determined to convince him.

She was interrupted by the arrival of a soldier, a man of about thirty, with short, neat hair and strong shoulders. The soldier stepped through the door, went straight to a chair, sat and faced them with hard eyes.

"Alright, somebody tell me what this whole thing is about," said the soldier.

Mayali waited for Joseph to speak, forgetting he could not. The boy just shuffled on his bare feet. The look of confusion on her face must have registered with the man and his face became gentle. "I apologize. I should introduce myself. I'm Lieutenant Kishan Dasrath of the Guyana Defense Force." The soldier pointed to Mayali, "And you are?"

In the past six months Mayali had used her mental power to help learn the local language to the point where she sounded like she had grown up speaking Creole. This officer spoke English, but it was easy to follow.

"I is Mayali," she told him. She assessed the soldier. He was confident, and his underlings obeyed him. She had planned to speak to their king or president or whatever he called himself and alert him of the Spider threat once she had established herself in this world, but now that the Brothers had arrived, she couldn't wait. Maybe this soldier was the best choice for revealing herself.

"Any other name?" Dasrath asked her.

"No. Just Mayali."

"And you?" he turned to Joseph.

"He can't talk," Mayali said.

"Ah, yes, I've heard about him." Dasrath turned back to Mayali. "Well, I've got my men looking at the church and the area around it with the police. But we're not finding anything and we need to know exactly what you saw."

"What is he saying?" Joseph wanted to know.

"Shut up," Mayali told him. *"I listening to—"*

"Just tell me."

But she spoke to Dasrath instead, using Creole. "Look, if I tell you the truth, you got fo' promise to listen to it. I mean, give me a chance fo' talk the whole thing, right?"

"Yes, very well."

Joseph stayed quiet and Mayali used the Touch to let him know what she heard as she heard it. She had never tried this before, but it worked well enough that Joseph seemed to be hearing the spoken conversation through her. The process seemed to make him grind his teeth in pain, however.

"The people who attack me at the church come from another place. Another world. Like there got a passage way to another land. A whole lot of passageway probably. I come from there. A land called Zolpash. That mean 'The place of sulphur'. It had another name before that, but long ago King Arrak and the rest of the Spider god come and wreck it and any other name don't matter no more." Mayali paused and saw that the soldier was looking at her soberly. This gave her hope. Maybe he believed her and would help.

"They does thief people from over here. They using them as slave and killing them out with the work, so they got to keep taking more people. And they make it so that it don't have water over there, so they thief that from here too."

"And you're one of them?" asked Dasrath.

"Me and me family, me whole village, they make us into slave. I get away and come here."

"How did you get here?" asked Dasrath calmly.

"They got a passageway up the river. I come through six month now. My father tell me about the passage. He born over here. The Spider kidnap he." Mayali produced an old ID card with a photo.

"I've seen you trying to paint that picture," Joseph said.

Mayali ignored him.

Dasrath copied the information from the card and gave it back, but only after Mayali demanded it.

"What kind of army does your world have?" Dasrath asked.

"Well, the real power is the Guatrachi – that mean fat ass people. That is the name that we does call the Spider."

"So, these Spider gods are real?" If the soldier was finding her tale unbelievable, it did not show on his face.

"Yes," said Mayali. "They real for sure. Sometime they make we line up behind one another in row and bow down to them. I see them me own self. They big. Big like a house!"

"And you escaped? How?"

"I had to wait til they open a passage. They can only do it when the moon line up the right way. I had help. The rockslider, that's the creature who live there before all the Spider and Snake, they help me. They say I must take back help. So I need you to help. The army can—"

"Wait, you say there are Snake gods too?"

"No. Not anymore. The Spiders had a big war with them and kill them out."

"How would the army be able to get over there to ... Sulphur Land you called it?" Dasrath asked.

"I don't know. I only come to tell you and to find my—"

The door opened and another soldier entered. After he whispered into Dasrath's ear, the lieutenant looked at Joseph with surprise and left the room, locking the door behind him.

"*You really believe all that stuff you're saying?*" Joseph asked.

"*Of course. Is the truth.*"

"*The Spider gods want to take over Guyana? The world here?*"

"*I think they want to take over everything, but they can't do much here as yet.*"

Lieutenant Dasrath walked back into the room his eyes red with anger. In one hand he carried Joseph's bag and cell phone. He pulled the laptop out and set it open on the counter then glowered at Joseph.

"This bag belongs to you. I've seen you with it. You been running that damned radio station. You telling people about how I's a drunkard. Got me running from bush to bush trying to find you,"

Dasrath shouted.

Mayali could understand the soldier better now that he was angry and using Creole. She felt a little sorry for the boy who wilted in the face of the soldier's wrath, until Dasrath turned to her.

"And you – you just fulla damn mischief and nonsense. Comin' in here telling me 'bout giant spider people coming to kill we."

"But, is—" Mayali said.

"I come to Mabaruma and work hard. I treat y'all people good. I don't take advantage pon them young girl; I don't call y'all 'buck man' and insult nobody. I deserve lil respect."

"Is not anything like—"

"Shut up." He looked her over as if she were a cockroach. "I don't believe nothing what you tell me. Nothing!"

Mayali never took well to being ordered around. "You can't tell me shut up! I talking the truth. You—"

Dasrath turned to his aide. "Lock them up. Don't let them talk to one another."

After a moment, he seemed to catch his composure becoming a professional again with his voice calm. "No food for the night either. I bet they tell me the truth in the morning, if they want their breakfast. I'm going to go talk to their parents in the meantime."

~ ~ ~ ∷ ~ ∶ ~ ∷ ~ ~ ~

Mayali found herself sharing a small, wooden room with a dented tin bucket holding a mop and a cabinet in the corner with a termite-eaten leg. She did not even have her knife. The soldiers had searched her and found it strapped to her lower back under her shirt.

"*Can you hear me?*" Joseph asked.

"*Yes. Where did they take you?*"

"Right down the hall from where we were. I'm in a cell with two miners. They're sleeping. They smell drunk."

"I can't imagine sleeping in a place like this."

"I thought you came from the Land of Sulphur and Suffering?"

"Yes," Mayali said. "I never slept well there either."

"Is anyone in there with you?"

Mayali told him, "No. This is a store room."

"They probably had to put you there since Dasrath said to separate us. How come your voice isn't so clear?"

"Because we not next to each other. The further we're apart, the less it works." Mayali inspected the floor. The wood looked loose in a few places, but she doubted it led anywhere. "Joseph, we have to get out of here."

"Once they catch the people who attacked us, they'll let us out of here. It might—"

"No, I mean we have to get out of Mabaruma. Or I do at least. You're always talking about the boat on your radio. Can you get me on there without anyone seeing?"

"It won't help for you to leave. You'll just look guilty."

"I don't care about that. I need to get to Georgetown." Mayali examined the walls, touching them with her fingertips. "My father is there. And the president. I have—"

"You can't just go meet the president! And why you think he would believe you if Dasrath didn't?"

"Because he's the president. He's smarter than everyone else." Malayi scanned the room while she waited for Joseph's response. "Joseph are you there?"

"Yes, yes. Sorry, I was laughing. I guess that doesn't travel over the Spider talk."

Malayi ignored him. She didn't see anything funny in what she said. Behind the cabinet, she found the wall was also eaten through by termites. She could see grass several feet below through the cracks.

She grabbed the mop handle and squeezed it between two boards at waist height. She worked the stick around slowly prying the boards off the corner support post.

"You know, you could just stay here and they'll listen to your story. If they put you in front of the magistrate, you can scream all you want about Spiders coming to invade." Joseph said.

"No. None of them have the authority to do anything. I need to talk to the man in charge of it all and that means getting to Georgetown."

Footsteps shuffled past her door. *"They brought food. But not for me,"* Joseph said. *"I think they threatened the miners to not share their food with me or else?"*

"Or else wha— ?"

"Mayali?"

Mayali ignored Joseph. The two guards had paused near her door. She strained to hear what they had to say, managing to catch a snatch of their conversation before they moved away.

"They found Father Garcia."

"Oh thank God. Is he alright?"

"They took him to the hospital. They were probably torturing him for information. He got stabbed and beat up. They don't know if he going to live."

"I should never have run. I should have helped him fight them."

"They would have just done the same—"

"You shouldn't have made me run away, Mayali."

"I didn't make you do anything."

No response. Footsteps tracked back the other way followed by silence.

Mayali continued to work at the boards. After about a half an hour, she was able to force two boards out at an angle. She stuck her head through. Below, a concrete sidewalk and an adjacent drain ran around the building. The drain was quarter-filled with stagnant, green water. There were a few buildings on this side of the compound, but no people. Dense trees stood past the fence and nothing but the setting sun beyond that.

An open window to the room next door was just three feet to her left. Mayali eased her torso through the gap in the wood and reached her fingers to the nearest sill. Using the frame, she pulled herself up and kicked off the opening she had made. She swung almost too far and lost her grip but was able to wrap her arm over the sill as she was about to fall. Grunting, she pulled herself over and onto the floor.

This room was an office and the door opened to a corridor. One end held a barred metal gate with voices beyond. The other end was a door locked with three large bolts. She slid the bolts open with care then pulled the door out a few inches. Light hit Joseph in the face.

"Ooaghh!" he yelped.

Mayali was glad he at least kept his voice low.

"Come quick," she told him.

"How did you get out?"

"I made myself a window. Come, let's go."

"I'm not going anywhere," Joseph said. *"I didn't do anything wrong."*

"Look, Dasrath went to find your parents. You think the Brothers won't know to look for them too? As long as I'm here, you and your family are in danger. Help me leave and you'll be safe."

"You don't need my help. Just get on the boat and go! And don't come back either." Joseph pushed her out of the door.

She marched straight back to the window and climbed onto the sill, looking for a way down. But the wood under her cracked and broke, spilling her downward. She was agile enough to stay upright, but her left foot landed on the sharp lip of the drain. Pain flared in her ankle causing her to cry out as she crumpled.

CHAPTER 3
No Phone, No Food, No Shoes

ayali?" Joseph called, hearing her curse in his head. *"Did something happen?"*

After a pause, her voice came back strained but even. *"I fell."*

"Bad?"

"Yes. I don't think I can walk right now."

Joseph left the cell and soon found the broken window. Mayali was struggling to stand below. What had the stupid girl done to herself now? She did seem to be in real pain, though. Joseph checked the window's sturdiness and dropped off the edge, landing at her side. She was sitting with her feet dangling over the drain, her jeans ripped in two places and her right sandal missing. The left ankle was red and purple. She gritted her teeth as he stooped near her.

"I tried to get up, but it hurts."

Joseph looked around. He was officially an escapee now, but no one had seen them yet. He scooped Mayali up under her shoulders and she twisted around in protest. Her lips moved, but all he noticed were the specks of mud spattered below her chin.

He held her up from under her right shoulder and he walked and Mayali hopped toward the wire mesh fence. Her breathing was heavy against his arm. There were spikes at the top of the fence but no barbed wire. With Joseph helping from below, Mayali eased herself over the top. She was halfway down the other side when she lost her footing and fell.

Joseph joined her quickly, helping her back to her feet. Together they walked and hobbled, working their way among the trees.

"I hear people coming," Mayali told him. *"We have to go faster."*

"You're the one slowing us down."

Mayali didn't answer.

"Are they still coming?" he asked her.

"Yes. They sound closer."

"Grab my neck," he told her, stooping with his back to her. She mounted him gingerly and he set off at a half-trot carrying her piggyback.

"They can still catch us at this speed," she said.

"No. It's basically jungle here. They'll have to stop and search and we can take a side path around the ridge."

Joseph had been walking the forest since he was a young boy bored with school and unable to make friends. His lone explorations had taught him all the routes and streams. The dark of the early night only hindered him a little but he forced Mayali to stop often and rest her foot, so it took hours for them to travel south to the edge of the river. Joseph sat Mayali between the roots of a tall tree.

"You have a phone?" he asked.

"No. Why?"

"So I can call my parents."

Joseph looked around, then down at Mayali. Her left ankle was swollen. *"Here, let me loosen your sandal."* She made no fuss as he did so. Afterward, they sat in silence for a while.

"We need food," Mayali said.

"We'll get food at the wharf. We just have to wait until morning."

Again, Mayali made no fuss. *"We'll need water before then."*

"You're right. We should move to a place with water."

"No. They'll check the streams tonight. It's where they would expect us to go."

"Well then I'll go get us some water before they arrive," Joseph said.

During the night they awoke to the distant movement of electric lights twisting about among the distant trees. Joseph wondered if it might not just be best to call the soldiers over but Mayali shook her head at him. He decided to stick with the plan – get her out of

Mabaruma and out of his life.

No one got near to them and they went back to sleep as the lights drifted away.

~ ~ ~ : : ~ : ~ : ~ : : ~ ~ ~

Unable to depend on the vibration of his phone, Joseph told Mayali to listen for the sound of his wristwatch alarm. It was set for six, but hunger pains woke him first. He opened his eyes to find Mayali staring out at the river through the trees. There was no wind just cool, still air. The water stood placid under the brightening day.

Joseph's belly grumbled.

"I'm so hungry."

Mayali ignored him, continuing to be hypnotized by the river.

"We might as well head to Kumaka," he said.

They walked again, Joseph barefoot, Mayali with a sandal on her good foot. The other ankle was too swollen. She tried breaking off a piece of branch to use as a staff, but could not muster the force needed. Joseph twisted it off for her and stripped the leaves. Even with Joseph and the branch for support, they still took an hour to walk the five hundred yards to the wharf. The ship grew larger alongside the dock as they edged their way along the paths near the water's edge. The original ferry landing was disused. Its high shed roof was tilted and twisted from neglect. The *Lady Northcote* was tied up at the supply wharf next door.

The ship was about a hundred and thirty feet long. It was compact and sturdy looking. The keel was dull black, rising to just above the dark water. The sides were rust-specked white, low at the middle, but rising to a plateau at the railed bow where a mast stood with a winch. The passenger cabin, one level above the main deck, took up the back half of the boat. The bridge rested upon it with the red smokestack rising behind. The letters T&HD were painted there inside a white diamond-shaped border – for 'Transport and Harbours Department'.

Travellers had assembled throughout the night and stalls were active on the road outside the wharf, selling liquor, cook-up rice, fried fish and fruits. Joseph could feel the bass vibrations from the loud music as the eight o'clock departure approached.

Three soldiers stood conspicuously at the steel-wire gate of the wharf, their guns on slings over their shoulders, talking to each other while they watched the passengers drift in. Joseph and Mayali moved around to the rear of the stalls, in the mud, grass and discarded garbage of the market, also watching the crowd.

"That's Jamesy walking on the deck," said Joseph. *"Lucky for us he's the captain this trip. He knows me from when I've traveled with Father Garcia. He lets us travel on the bridge with him."*

Mayali asked, *"So what now?"*

"We need tickets for the boat, but those soldiers are in front of the office and— Oh, no."

"What?"

"Tara." He pointed to a girl a little older than them checking through denim skirts at a stall. Her curly, black hair was loose, falling past a sprinkling of small star tattoos on her neck. She was that indefinable mix of black, Amerindian and Portuguese that the mining industry had created with its influx of people. She claimed her father was Venezuelan, but no one Joseph knew had ever met the man.

"Who's that?" Mayali asked.

"My girlfriend."

"You have a girlfriend?" Mayali looked back at Joseph and then at the girl.

"Yes," said Joseph. *"I can't have a girlfriend?"*

"So, how do you, um, talk?"

"I can operate a radio show. Communicating with one girl isn't that

hard."

Mayali smirked. *"I bet the only way you met her is through that radio show."*

Joseph looked away, but Mayali wasn't interested in his embarrassment. She said, *"Get Tara to help you."*

"I can't," said Joseph. *"She's going to ask too many questions. Let me write you a note—"*

"Tara," Mayali called, throwing an empty can at the girl. Joseph could hear the words through the Spider's Touch.

When Tara saw them, her eyes grew alarmed and then angry. She marched over, still holding a skirt on a clothes hanger, and poked Joseph in the chest with a finger. "Where you been?" she asked, her words penetrating to Joseph through Mayali's ears. "Why you ain't answering your phone?"

Joseph put his finger to his lips and tapped them frantically. He looked over to the soldiers. They had not noticed.

"I been calling you whole night. No reply. Now you walking with some strange girl."

Joseph grunted and signalled her with his palms to be quiet again.

"You don't even have on shoes. What—"

Mayali asked, "The army people didn't say nothing about us?"

"No," said Tara. "Why? What happen?"

"Don't tell her," Joseph said. *"Dasrath must be keeping it secret because he's embarrassed that we got away."*

Mayali said, "Joseph need your help. It very important."

Tara looked at her with a raised eyebrow. "And you is who?"

"He trying to help me. I got fo' go to Georgetown on the boat and we can't let them soldier see we."

"Why? One of them is you boyfriend or something?"

"Tell her yes," Joseph said. *"Tell her he's very jealous."* Malayi complied.

"Yeah, that is how them soldier-boy does be," Tara said, "always trying to get some young girl for they self." Tara looked at Joseph. "So what I got fo' do?"

"Buy two ticket for we," Mayali said.

"Yeah, alright." Tara stretched out her palm and waited.

"We don't got any money right now. Joseph going to pay you back later."

Tara's nostrils flared and she gave Joseph a sour look. He gave her an I-can't-help-it shrug. She smiled and said, "Alright. But make sure you pay me back."

She also bought them some food along with the tickets – stale chow-mien from Mr. de Santos' food shop. They ate it almost instantly. Tara also brought some ice in a plastic bag for Mayali's foot. She told them they could have that for free since it came from her sister's bar.

They found a handcart of plantains waiting to be loaded onto the ship and drove it around a corner, out of sight. It was made from an open wooden tray about four feet across with large tyres and long handles for pushing. Mayali got beneath the plantains on the floor of the cart. Joseph tucked his long hair under a floppy fisherman's hat Tara had borrowed. She had also found him a gray long-sleeved shirt with a tear in one elbow. Holding a ticket in one hand, she walked straight for the gate. Joseph pushed the cart behind her. He kept his face down.

While Tara spoke to the young soldiers about the Village Party planned for the next month, Joseph pushed past them on the other side, his heart da-da-dumping hard enough for him to feel it up his neck. He parked the cart near a corner of the brick-walled shed that served as the passenger waiting room. Everyone else was seated on benches facing the water. When Joseph was sure no one would see, he told Mayali to climb out. They sat among the passengers on the waiting benches and boarded when the gangway to the ship was lowered.

The ship smelled of diesel and smoke and rust. The slight concave shape of the main deck forced them into uneven, short steps as they walked to the main stairs. On the middle level, everyone was spreading out to the rails and the forward balcony or else they were setting up camp inside the long bench-lined passenger seating area.

Joseph led Mayali to the ladder-like stairs leading to the bridge. Joseph went first, looking around for Jamesy at the top. There was a man in clean, work clothes right in front of him. The man faced the bow with his back to them. Joseph could tell it was not Captain Mackenzie. He stopped and Mayali bumped into him causing him to collide with the man who was not Captain Mackenzie.

The man turned and spoke in a clear, stern voice. "What are you doing up here?" Despite his trimmed beard and combed hair, the man appeared dangerous as his eyes bulged.

"We travelling with the captain," said Mayali at Joseph's prompting.

"No, you're not. I am the captain of this vessel."

"But, we saw Captain Mackenzie down—"

"Listen me!" the man said, his voice low and serious. "I am Captain McWatt. I don't allow anyone on my bridge who has no business here. Leave at once."

Defeated, they descended to the main cabin. Some of the regular travellers had already strung up hammocks to claim their bit of the room. Others were napping upright in their seats. All the excited first-timers and children were at the rails, front and stern.

"You made it to the boat in any case," Joseph said. *"I have to go now. I'll tell Dasrath you ran away south to the airstrip so they won't search the boat."*

Mayali nodded and followed him out to the front rail. As he set one foot to go down, however, Mayali said, *"Stop. The Brothers are here."*

"How do you know?"

"I can hear them talking." She pointed to the shore at the side of

the wharf.

A man in an ordinary brown shirt was talking to a watermelon vendor. The man was pointing at the watermelons while the vendor was shaking his head and arguing back.

"That's their trick," said Mayali. *"They can't really talk. But they have a power to suggest things. They always ask if a person is obeying the rules and then that person's conscience makes them imagine some authority they fear."*

"That's why I saw him as a radio inspector?"

"Yes."

"For everyone else, they just see a person in plain clothes. Nobody special."

The wharf attendant unhooked the bow line and tossed it to a waiting sailor who leaned out to catch it then started winding it in.

"So what do they really look like?" Joseph asked.

"Listen for them and you can hear them."

"I know what they sound like. I'm asking what they really look like."

"Listen for them and once you hear their voice, you can focus on them and see through the illusion."

Joseph stretched out to hear the Brother in his mind. The words started as a fizzy whisper and grew. *"... require you to follow the law. You know that fruits must be displayed at least twenty inches from the ground...."* When Joseph ignored the voice and tried to see the speaker, really see him, there was a sensation of a blink and he could see the red-robed figure from the church tower, head beneath a cowl, fuzzy fingers peeking out of the long, loose sleeves.

"How can I see what's under those robes?"

"You can't. That's what they're really wearing."

The ship's horn blasted out a loud but mellow sound. It was ready to depart. Joseph started to leave.

"You can't leave. The Brother will see you. He will know I'm on the ship."

"He already suspects it. He's going to investigate it anyway."

"If he catches you, he's going to get the truth from you much quicker than if he has to look around."

"I wouldn't tell him—"

"You think so? That one in red is Brother Hakk. He's the commander of the Brothers where I used to live. He's famous for torturing people's eyes. Can you imagine yourself strapped down flat, with a knife-point right above your eye, ready to stab you? Do you think you would really hold back anything?"

Joseph shuddered. He was dizzy from the Spider's Touch and his head was hurting. Clumsily, because of her ankle, Mayali led him away to the passenger cabin where he sat, holding his head. After about five minutes, he felt the ship start moving, picking up speed. Joseph leaned forward and vomited between his bare feet. As he strained to keep anything else from coming up, *Lady Northcote* set off for Georgetown.

CHAPTER 4
Spiders, Serpents and Turtles

"*Why are you so fascinated by that rainbow?*" Mayali heard Joseph ask as she faced the wind at the rails of the main deck. He was enjoying the wind with her, his hair loose and lifting behind him. They had been under way for two hours and his nausea had passed. In her mind, Mayali could still smell the stink of cleaning up his vomit with a shovel borrowed from one of the farmers.

Mayali was gazing west at the slice of colours that hung between two clouds. "*We never had rainbows where I come from,*" she said. "*We never had rain. No rivers either. Not even trees, because—*"

"*Where you come from sounds terrible.*"

She ignored him.

Joseph pointed at six white canvas bags of plantains on the deck near them. He said, "*I think those are the plantains you were hiding under.*"

Mayali shrugged and watched the bow wave run by in a curl at the boat's side, the crest swaying like a ribbon of white on the black river.

"*I'm getting hungry,*" Joseph said wandering over to the bags. "*I wonder if these are any good.*"

"*If you're going to take one, do it fast.*"

"*I'm not going to steal a plantain,*" Joseph snapped.

"*Then why bother checking them?*"

"*I don't know. Just wondering.*"

The rainbow was fading as the sun rose toward midday. To her right, Joseph was telling her to look at something, but she kept her eyes on the last of the rainbow. Weather was so peaceful here compared with home, even the storms. She had stood outside one midnight as the heavy drops exploded against her in the windswept dark and felt like she was being pelted by life itself. At home, everyone hid when the hardwater shards fell from the cloudfires, and any kind of wind made the crystals into little flying blades.

"I said look what I found in the bag," Joseph said, breaking into her thoughts. He was slowly removing his hand from the bag, a hairy black spider covering his palm. *"It's a tarantula. They're actually not dangerous. It must have been in-between the bunch since the farm. I wonder—"*

Mayali jumped at him, her mind panicked at the thought of that great beast so close to her the entire time she had been in the cart. She struck his hand as hard as she could. The spider popped into the air and over the side spinning away into the river.

Joseph looked at her with shock. *"Why'd you do that? I told you it wasn't dangerous."*

"Spiders are always dangerous. You can't ever trust them."

"This isn't the same place you came from. You have to understand that. This is God's land and His creation is good."

"I don't know if your God is real, but if he is, he made Zolpash too. And he made the Spiders. And that means he made evil and suffering."

Joseph glared at her then looked out over the water, brushing his hair away from his face.

Mayali turned toward him. *"Father Garcia always said boys should have short hair. You have long hair."*

"Well, he's wrong about that one. Samson had long hair. Even Jesus. All the pictures show it."

"Those are just paintings," Mayali said. *"I can make anyone look like anything when I paint."*

"Actually, the scripture—"

"Does Father Garcia know about Tara?"

"Yes," Joseph said, his jaw clenched.

"Does he know the two of you are committing sins of the flesh?"

"I never told you—"

"Does he?"

Joseph walked away, towards the ship canteen. Mayali watched him leave, wondering why she had brought up Father Garcia while the man was probably dying. After watching a particularly large and green tree drop out of view behind the ship, she limped after Joseph. He had all the money and she needed water.

Joseph bought her the water without speaking to her, then left for the stern. Again, she followed. The stern of the lower deck was surprisingly close to the water. A waist-high, curved wall of steel separated her from the churning white water of the ship's wake. The bark of a dog attracted her attention.

"*Look. Captain Mackenzie,*" Joseph said pointing to the man sitting on a bench next to a brown dog with a pink collar. The dog was medium-sized and was lying with its head on a camouflage travel bag, looking up at them. A long leather case was on the bench next to it.

The man waved at Joseph and called them over.

"I know Joseph don't talk. How about you?"

"I does talk."

"Oh, good. Well, good morning." He waved his hand to the seat across from him and they sat. Joseph offered a handshake and Captain Mackenzie took it. The dog continued watching them, tongue hanging out. Up close, Mayali could see it had a blaze of white on its chest.

Mayali was not sure if she should be shaking this stranger's hand, so she just said, "Morning."

"*Call him Captain Mackenzie,*" Joseph told her. "*You can't just talk to him without respect.*"

"Ah, morning, Captain Mackenzie," she said. "You not driving the boat today?"

The man gave a puzzled smile and said, "Just call me Jamesy."

"Okay. Morning, Jamesy."

Jamesy smiled again. "I on leave. I just travelling home as a passenger today. I was in the bush with some friends, hunting."

"*Ask him if that's why he has a gun,*" Joseph said.

"*What gun?*"

"That long case has a gun inside."

The captain knitted his eyebrows as he watched them.

"That is your gun?" Mayali asked. The case was black and oblong, giving no clue of the contents.

"Yeah," said Jamesy, patting the case. "Is a .308 calibre. Is good for shooting deer. You get some nice big ones up here. Not so much nowadays like when I first start hunting, but they still got good meat."

They spent the rest of the morning talking about ways to hunt for deer and other animals, the way things worked on the ship, Jamesy's friends in Mabaruma and other stories about his life. He never asked about their trip, though he seemed like he wanted to several times; instead he let their questions lead the conversation.

At lunch time, he offered to buy them food and Mayali accepted despite Joseph telling her it was impolite.

The dog had gotten friendlier and friendlier to Joseph as the conversation went on and soon it was letting him pet his head and shoulders. The captain stopped him from giving the dog part of his lunch, saying that Daisy had already eaten.

"He name Daisy?" Mayali asked.

"Yeah."

"But he's a boy dog."

"I know, but me wife and me did want a daughter long and we end up never getting children. So when I carry home the dog, she say he name Daisy and that was it."

"He does behave very good," Mayali said. There were no dogs in her world and the boisterousness of the strays she had met in Mabaruma made her fearful.

"Yeah, he know how to be quiet. Especially in the bush."

"The bush is dangerous for dogs," Joseph said.

"It safe to take him?" Mayali asked.

"Well, he know to stay near me all the time. We only ever get into trouble one time."

"What happen?"

"Daisy went to drop a load in the bush and the next thing I know he come running and barking straight back into camp with this jaguar chasing he. I was the only one around and the jaguar must be not see me, and it trying to get Daisy and they run down to the river. There had a tree trunk fall and stick out over the water and Daisy end up there, but he realize he would get catch if he jump in the water, so he spin right around. The jaguar climb up behind he and in Daisy eye you can see like he know he gon' dead but he decide he won't dead easy."

Jamesy looked at the dog who was lying there calmly with his ears up. "Daisy barking loud and growling and howling and showing all he teeth and even snapping at the jaguar and you could see the jaguar look confused. Like it never expect anything to fight back. Daisy actually back it up to the edge of the trunk, but I had me gun out by then and I put a bullet in the wood between them and break up the whole thing."

"Why you didn't just kill it?" Mayali asked. "I thought you say you was a good hunter."

"You can't shoot a jaguar like that!" Joseph said.

"They got rules about that," Jamesy said. "Endangered species they call it. Besides, the jaguar wouldn't have keep fighting."

"But the jaguar would have win."

"Yes, but it know Daisy might have hurt it, and if the jaguar get hurt bad enough it wouldn't be able to hunt and then it gon' die. Animal not stupid. They don't fight unless is to survive."

The spaces between the tree trunks grew darker and the topmost leaves flared with yellow light as the sun eased down to the west. The river widened too. Mayali felt everything shift as the *Lady Northcote* swung herself right and curved out along the coast. Being at the back of the ship, it seemed to Mayali as if the sea magically appeared.

"It don't seem possible that water can just go on forever," Mayali said, watching sunlight glint off the wave tops. The rippled water seemed playful and warm.

"You never see the ocean before?" Jamesy asked.

"No, I only—" The ship swayed in the higher waves and the disorientation of watching water stretching to the sky gave her the sensation of the parts of her body being disconnected from each other, like leaves on a tree. She felt dizzy and took rapid, panicked breaths.

"Sit down, sit down." She felt Jamesy and Joseph placing her back on the bench, but she never took her eyes off the line in the distance, sometimes sharp and sometimes melting away.

Captain Mackenzie patted her on the shoulder and said, "I been in this business a long time. I won't tell you me age, but I almost old like this ship and this ship seventy-five years old. And even now, sometime I see the water in the ocean and it make me dizzy too."

As the afternoon wore on, Jamesy brought out a pack of cards. He and Joseph got straight to it with a few of the other passengers, using a suitcase as the card table. Mayali watched from nearby as Joseph seemed to win quite a bit.

When the game broke up an hour later, she asked him how he could play so well.

"I learned with my friends. You don't need to talk to play cards, so that's something we did a lot. I found out I'm good at it. It's almost like I can see what's coming in the deck sometimes because of how people play. It's like I can rearrange them in my head to make sense."

Captain Mackenzie bought them dinner as well that day. To their left the shore passed in absolute darkness, no lights among the trees. To the seaward, a few small fishing boats revealed themselves with the kerosene lamps they used to set their lines. As the night turned cold a sailor came around the outside of the ship, dropping blue tarpaulins from the ceiling like blinds to shield the passengers from the night wind. Jamesy went over to chat.

Mayali could not hear the conversation, but she could see the sailor look over at her a few times as he did most of the talking. Twice,

Jamesy glanced their way.

The dog was sitting at their feet eating fried chicken from a styrofoam box just like theirs. When Joseph finished off his first piece of meat, he leaned down and gave Daisy the bone. The dog crunched into it with a little growl and ate it all.

"You should give him your bones too," Joseph said.

"Why?" Mayali looked at the dog, who seemed to be smiling up at her. She had been considering eating the bone herself. She had learned long ago that everything was edible when food was scarce.

"Just give it to him." Joseph gave the dog his other bone.

Daisy took a few minutes to eat it and then looked up at Mayali again. She checked that there was no meat left on her bones and then leaned carefully down, half expecting Daisy to bite at her hand. The dog stayed politely seated until she had dropped the gifts into his bowl, then he devoured them.

There was a strange sensation of pride in Mayali's stomach as she watched the animal eat the food she had given it. Suddenly, she liked the dog a lot more.

Joseph hopped onto the rail of the ship, and sat with one knee drawn up to his chest and one leg dangling over the side, nothing but blackness beyond him as the tarpaulins flapped with whumping sounds nearby.

"You have good balance," Mayali said, her tone friendly. She climbed gingerly up and mirrored him on the other side of their section of railing, bracing her back against the post, her injured ankle hanging free. *"I don't usually meet other people who like heights."*

"Is that why you're always climbing trees? For the height?"

"I told you, we don't have trees where I come from. Being in one is amazing."

"Father Garcia says that most people who go deaf from an injury lose their sense of balance because of the damage. For some reason my accident made my balance even better."

"Father Garcia is a helpful man," Mayali said. *"He taught you how to use sign language?"*

"Yes. I wasn't learning anything in school and I was too young to go to the special school in Georgetown. Father Garcia, he taught himself sign language just so he could teach it to me. Now that my friends aren't around anymore, he's the only one around I can talk to."

"Something happened to your friends?"

"I didn't have a lot to start with," Joseph said. *"Then they all dropped out of school to go work in the gold pits. One of them died when the sides of the pit fell in. Jonas. He was only sixteen. That's why my father said I couldn't go with them. If you can't hear, you'll get into all kinds of accidents."*

"So you don't play cards any more?"

"I play strip poker with Tara sometimes."

"What's that?"

"Never mind," Joseph said.

"Tell me."

"Well, usually you play the game for money, but with strip poker you play for each other's clothes."

"That doesn't make sense," said Mayali. *"You can't wear her clothes if you win them."*

"The point is just to get the other person out of their clothes."

"What? Why would—" Mayali smiled. *"Oh, right."*

"Right."

After a few seconds, Mayali said *"We had a game like that too."*

"Really?"

"Yes. If I liked a boy I would take him by the hand and walk somewhere private and dark and we would kiss."

"That doesn't sound much like a game," said Joseph.

"Exactly. I don't see why you need to play a game to see your girlfriend naked."

"I don't need the game. The game is just fun. Don't you understand

fun? Or is that why you stopped at kissing? You never did anything more?"

Mayali shrugged. *"Nothing all the way. There's stuff in-between kissing and sex."*

"Yeah," said Joseph wickedly. "In-between your le—"

Joseph blinked and dismounted the rail.

"Getting dizzy again?" Mayali asked.

"Yes. Not as bad as before, but this Spider Talk isn't easy."

Mayali let him have silence.

"That's Shell Beach," Joseph said. Near the shore a string of lights had appeared, isolated like a constellation of stars fallen from the sky. *"That's where the giant turtles nest"*

"Turtles were the first Lords of the universe," Mayali said by reflex.

"What?"

"Before the Serpent of Many Colours wrapped creation inside its coils and sent its children to rule over the many worlds, the Turtles put the planets, stars and moons in their places and set them in motion."

"Is that from a book?"

"We don't have books where I come from. It's from a story we tell children. My father knew a lot of the stories even though he wasn't born in Zolpash." Pointing at the shore, she asked, *"Why does the turtle beach have lights?"*

"There's a conservation station there. They try to keep the turtles safe from people who want to eat them or eat their eggs."

"Why stop people from eating them? Are they only food for powerful people? We have that at home. Only Brothers can eat coconuts. I used to have to steal them. I bet turtle tastes good. I'd like to try it."

"No, the turtles are dying out. You really don't understand this endangered species thing, do you? You just said turtles were gods and now you want to eat them?"

"People need to eat. Gods will do just as well as any other animal."

CHAPTER 5
Swimming Lessons

Captain Mackenzie came over and took his seat. He gave both of them a serious look which made Joseph nervous. "I think is time the two of you tell me the truth about what going on," Jamesy said.

Almost as soon as the back half of Joseph's brain was telling his feet to run, the front half of his brain put a stop to it because there was nowhere to run.

"What you want to know?" Mayali asked before Joseph's thoughts had settled themselves.

"Don't tell him anything," he said to Mayali.

Mayali ignored him.

"Father Garcia was stabbed. Did you two have anything to do with that?"

Joseph vigorously shook his head no.

"Yes," Mayali said.

Captain Mackenzie looked sympathetic. "What happened?"

"Don't tell him," Joseph said, trying to stand between the other two. Daisy stood, tense.

Mayali stepped to the side, wincing as her ankle took her weight. She said to Jamesy. "Some dangerous people looking for me and they hurt Father Garcia."

"And what they want with you?"

"They think they own me."

A look of recognition was on Jamesy's face. "I know about that kind of thing. A lot of them mining camps does put young girls to work like that. You get away from them?"

"Yes. I get away long ago, but they ain't give up yet."

"Why? You thief from them or something?"

"Yes."

Joseph wondered why he was still surprised to hear this. Clearly, Mayali had been a renegade in her own world.

"But nothing serious," the girl said. "They just ain't ordinary people is all."

"Not ordinary, eh?" he asked knowingly. "That's why Joseph can understand what people saying all of a sudden?"

The two teens looked at each other, alarmed.

Jamesy laughed. "Is not hard to see. You better be careful from now on. Other people gon' notice."

Joseph nodded.

"So you running away?" Jamesy asked.

"Yes, plus I trying to find my—"

"No!" Joseph interrupted, loud enough this time to make Mayali stop. *"Don't tell him the rest. Don't forget that Dasrath was believing us and then said we were fooling him."*

"That was only because he found out you'd been making fun of him on the radio. He believed me."

"It doesn't matter. Jamesy thinks you're talking about miners. Leave it at that. You can't expect people to just believe about spiders and reading people's minds. I still don't believe half of what you tell me."

Mayali turned to Jamesy. "When I say that these people not ordinary, you understand what I mean, right?"

Jamesy looked serious. "I know. I grow up in the bush with me granny. Ever since I little she teach me about Kanaima and Moongazer and spirit and all kind of strange thing that live out there."

"You see?" Mayali said to Joseph. *"He believes me."*

"Fine. But I don't think you're being safe. You keep telling people these stories and they'll lock you up for being crazy." Joseph walked to the rail, looking out at the dark horizon and wondering about dinner back at his house. What were his parents doing to find him? He had to find a way to contact them.

The silence behind him interrupted his thoughts. Mayali was watching him, biting her lip. After a while, Jamesy spoke. "Alright, well is time for sleep."

Joseph walked with Mayali to the front of the ship for some water. "You didn't tell him," he said.

Mayali did not reply. As they walked, they saw the travellers bedding down on the benches and in their hammocks, some just using bags for pillows, others pulling out pillows and wrapping themselves in blankets. One couple snuggled a baby between them. The ship was much more still. Hardly anything moved and the vibration of the floor felt more distinct than ever.

"You haven't actually told me about your world," Joseph said, lying on a bench. Daisy had curled into a circle against him. Joseph had borrowed Jamesy's phone to play Hungry Birds, but he was still distracted by thoughts of his parents and Father Garcia.

"It's dry and it's hot. What else do you need to know?"

"Who are these Brothers? Why are they called Brothers?"

"They call themselves Brothers." Sarcastically, Mayali said, *"Us Dayan women, they call Sisters."*

"Dayan?"

Mayali said, *"The Spiders always mix up Spider blood with people . The Brothers are part Spider. But they can only be born from a Dayan woman, a woman who has the Spider's Touch. No one knows who'll be born a Dayani. It happens and the Spiders eventually test all the girls when they're old enough. Dayan women are kept in special dormitories all their lives. They have to bear children to create more Brothers."*

"They force you to have sex with them?"

"Hah! Like they could. No. Their equipment can't get hard. You know, down there?"

"Then how is it possible for—"

"The Spider way. They kind of pee it out at this station and then the Spiders bring in the Dayani and—"

"Okay, I think I get the idea," Joseph said, embarrassed.

"The Brothers can hardly stand to see a woman, much less touch one. Dayani have to wear clothes that cover them entirely, like long gowns before the Brothers visit."

Joseph looked her over for signs of monstrosity. *"So you want me to believe you're part Spider?"*

"Just a little part. Not like the Brothers, though. Once they come of age, the Spiders give the Brothers a special bite and they transform. With Dayani, we mostly just have the Touch."

Joseph stopped playing his video game and trying to judge how possible all this was. *"Why would they want to mix people with Spiders? Your story doesn't make sense."*

"It's true! The Brothers help them rule Zolpash with the Spider powers they get from the mixing. Arrak, the King of the Spiders, he and all his Lords keep our people working. Thousands of Spiders. They claim that they're eternal and that's why there aren't any female spiders. They don't need to breed. Females are a sign of weakness in a species they say."

"Why would they need people to work for them?" Joseph asked. *"It doesn't make sense."*

"You're talking to me in your mind and you're still doubting me?"

"Well, maybe I went as crazy as you and I'm imagining things."

Mayali shook her head sorrowfully. *"I wish I was lying. I wish these thing never—"*

"You're not answering me. What do the Spiders use your people for?"

"Building. Always building. The Spiders, they were losing the war against the Snakes. So Arrak created a spell that transformed the world. All the liquid became hard, like glass. Without liquid the Snake gods had no venom and they were destroyed. All that's left of them are their unbreakable skins. We take them and make houses."

"What about the Spider's venom?" Joseph asked. *"That would have*

dried up too."

"That's why they have to build. They came from this world, so they knew the way back and they found more portals and built stations to suck liquid water into Zolpash. So they always have enough to make venom."

"So your people make these stations?"

"We make everything. Like the roads. Hardwater falls in pieces that you can grind into powder and eat and it nourishes you. But the Spiders made huge machines for crushing hardwater and laying it out as sheets. We build roads with them, great curving things. If you climb high enough, you can see them like threads all over the land, connected one to another. The Spiders have these things like ships that they slide across the roads to get from one place to another."

Joseph's skeptical questions got him more information. Mayali's father had been kidnapped from Earth and enslaved. He had ended up living with a woman who bore him a child. Their home life was hard, with both parents committed to the Spiders' work, but Mayali had a father like no other child and he enjoyed telling his daughter stories.

Her father escaped when Mayali was ten, finding a way to use a portal back to earth. The chance had come so suddenly that he had only time to send a message with a friend for his family, telling them he would return when he could for them.

"We waited four years," said Mayali, eyes down. *"He didn't come. And then I got identified as a Dayani and the Brothers came to take me. Most people would just go when they were called. I knew my father wouldn't want that for me, so I ran. I watched from a mountain while my mother died holding them back. And then I kept going. The rocksliders found me nearly dead and took me to their caves."*

Jalana and her people had continued to resist the Spiders, hiding underground where reserves of liquid water kept them alive. The tale of her father's escape had inspired a plan in Jalana, the rockslider leader, and Mayali had come to Earth with their help on the condition that she let the leaders of earth know of the Spider threat and bring back the armies of Earth to fight the Spiders.

Joseph still hadn't gotten all his questions answered when he fell asleep, phone in hand.

He awoke during the night to the howling of a rainstorm. The ship's motion changed to a plunging, twisting ride. Despite the tarpaulins, the wind was spraying water about and he was cold. Daisy had cuddled himself tighter to Joseph's chest. Being too tired to care about getting wet, Joseph fell back asleep, the dog's breath in his face.

Jamesy woke them at dawn and offered them coffee from his personal flask, splitting his one man-sized serving into three small portions.

"So I hear you meet Captain McWatt." Jamesy said.

"He very sour," Mayali said.

Jamesy laughed. "Yeah. But he's a good man. He train in Cyprus. He take this captain thing very serious." He dug in his pockets. "When you get to Georgetown," Jamesy said, "make sure you buy some shoe. All two of you." He handed Mayali a wad of money which she put away without counting.

They were almost at Georgetown, the city's low buildings thickening the horizon to the south-east.

"There's a boat coming." Joseph tapped Jamesy's shoulder and pointed at the white water spraying as the large speedboat approached. It was a foreign import, not a locally made wooden boat.

"Coastguard," said Jamesy.

"No, not coastguard," said Mayali. "Is them. The people looking for me."

"You sure?"

Mayali didn't answer. Instead she turned to Joseph. *"You text anybody last night?"*

"Well, yes. I had to let my parents and Tara know I was okay."

"Like you stupid? You don't realize they watching them? They read your message."

"How?"

"These people can go everywhere. Everywhere!"

The coastguard boat, police lights flashing now, was close enough for Joseph to make out ten or so people aboard. He could also feel a buzzing in his head, gaining strength as the boat approached. It was the Spider's Touch and it hurt. The police boat pulled alongside the *Lady Northcote* and ordered a sailor to tie them alongside.

"Y'all have to hide. Come with me."

Jamesy took them to a large metal door with a circular handle. It opened to a ladder that dropped half a level. Joseph went last, holding Mayali steady as she hopped down on her good foot. At the bottom, Joseph felt thunderous vibrations from the engine from the ship's sole working engine. The engine room smelled of oil fumes and rust. Mayali looked like the noise was deafening her. There was a strong, shirtless man tending the engine. Captain Mackenzie spoke into his ear and the man nodded then pointed Joseph and Mayali into a corner. Jamesy left.

"I don't think it's safe to hide," Mayali said.

"Jamesy will keep them away. He has a gun."

"Help me get to those oil cans."

"Why? I'm not—"

"Sister!" a loud voice said in Joseph's head. "Sister, you must come with us. King Arrak demands it."

Mayali hobbled across the floor and tumbled an oil drum to the ground. Oil streamed across the floor. Joseph saw the engineer scream at her. She opened her lighter and set the oil on fire. Joseph ran to stamp it out, but the flames and heat sprang up fast and drove him back. The engineer hit the alarm button and ran for the fire extinguisher. Mayali dumped more oil on the floor, even with Joseph struggling to stop her.

"We have to go! Get us out!" Mayali shouted at Joseph.

"You do craziness and now I got fo save we?" Joseph pushed her up the ladder harder then he needed to and followed her onto the deck. Passengers were running for the front of the *Lady Northcote* while sailors yelled at them to calm down and put on life jackets.

"See?" Mayali said. *"This is what Jamesy was talking about last night when he was telling us about what they do if there's a fire. They're going to make everybody get in the front. The Brothers won't be able to search for us."*

"The fire is going to go out soon."

"They're going to have to shut down the engine. But in the meantime, we're getting closer to the shore. We just have to wait."

"So you actually have a plan?" Joseph asked.

"No." Mayali grabbed his shoulder and directed him to take them up to the passenger deck and then forward. They saw Captain McWatt trying to organize the passengers, his back turned to them. Joseph helped Mayali climb up to the stairs to the bridge. The sailor steering the big wheel was too intent on the front of the boat to notice them. Behind the bridge was the roof above the passenger cabins, an open black space broken only by the large red exhaust funnel and four lifeboats, and smoke leaking out from underneath.

As they edged across it, Joseph could feel Mayali wincing extra hard with each step on her injured ankle. The engine vibrations ceased. They were drifting up the Demerara river now. To their left were wharves and the city itself beyond the red roofs of the Stabroek Market. The market wharf at the riverside seemed ready to fall down, resting on wooden piles narrowed in the middle by time to half their original width.

They ducked behind the lifeboat when Mayali heard the captain. He was arguing with a Brother who had followed him and Joseph smiled as he heard it. "Sir," McWatt said disdainfully, "I am the captain of this vessel and we are in an emergency. You are to leave this bridge at once and not bother me. Keep your men with the passengers."

"That should give us some time," Mayali said, amused.

The voice of the Brother broke into Joseph's mind. *"You are still trapped Sister. We will find you. Our anger will be less if you come to us of your own volition."*

"Isn't there a way to block him out?" Joseph asked. They crawled through smoke to the back of the ship as it drifted closer to the shore. Twenty feet below them, the wake of the *Lady Northcote* had gone quiet.

"We have to jump," Mayali said.

"From up here? No way. Let's climb down to the next level at least."

"My ankle can't take that. We have to jump before those idiots find a way to get to us."

Mayali grabbed Joseph's wrist and leapt off. Joseph felt his face stiffen in fear and then they hit, Mayali with her bad leg folded away from the water, him painfully on his side. Immediately Mayali was in his head telling him to swim. She was weighing him down, and his head was in pain from an over load of the Spider's Touch and now she wanted him to just swim ashore?

"You have to help," he said to her.

"How?"

He was about to tell her to kick with her feet, but she was too injured. And splashing her arms about would just slow them down. He said, *"Take deep breaths and cover your nose."*

He twisted behind her, grabbing her across the chest with his arm under her shoulders. With his free arm and his legs, he swam backwards, losing track of time as he hunted for breath. He could see the ship getting further and further away. He kicked blindly, hoping that he was moving the right way. It made his muscles ache and his breaths got shorter and more painful.

His head hit something hard. He turned and the water's motion drove his face into one of the wharf piles. He coughed, and his grip on

Mayali slipped.

"What? What happened?" she asked.

But Joseph was losing his control and his legs didn't respond when he ordered them to kick. Panic rose in his throat as he sank lower. He reached about wildly with his hands, but couldn't grip anything. A ladder dropped down from above. A young face was looking down at them and Mayali was saying, *"Climb."*

Still gasping, Joseph helped Mayali up, careful of her ankle. One after the other, they emerged through a section of the wharf where the floorboards were missing. Dozens of people were huddled around, asking them questions in a jumble, but something exploded out on the ship and the spectators ran back to the edge of the wharf to look.

Mayali and Joseph sat flat, staring at the boy, who had stayed at their side. He was a few years younger than them, with short, curly hair and a missing front tooth. His dirty T-shirt was too big for him, hanging like a scarecrow prop while his trunks were too small, and barely showed from under the shirt hem.

He pulled the ladder up, saying, "You lucky Miss Jackie does keep this around fo' stack she rice pon top she stall. Got to clean the mud off or she gon' know I thief it and—"

Mayali rose to her knees, one hand holding her ankle. *"They coming again,"* she said.

CHAPTER 6

The Prince of the Garden City

Mayali saw the Coast Guard boat break away from the smoking, drifting *Lady Northcote*, but the buzz of the Spider's Touch was too heavy to be coming from the Brothers in the boat. She looked around. To the left was water and a dock full of shipping containers. Ahead were the market's stalls and deep, unlit corridors, bubbling with sound, but with no sign of Brothers. To the right was the T&HD wharf, judging by the letters she recognized though she could not read them. It was also connected to the market. The water between the two wharves was filled with a cacophony of coloured speedboats emptying and taking on passengers at a precarious looking platform. Within the unceasing movement of people, three men stood, looking at them. Brothers.

Why were they standing still? Mayali looked around. Two other Brothers were sneaking along the concrete wall on the river's edge, coming at them.

"Them people coming for you?" the boy who had helped them asked.

"Yes," said Mayali. "They trying to kill we."

"Well you better run fast." The boy took off and Joseph ran after him. Mayali looked back at the Coast Guard boat – still coming fast – and then she limped as fast as she could into the market. The cracked, unpainted, wooden deck of the wharf changed to the chipped, unpainted, concrete floor of the corridors. Mayali lost track of the Brothers as she walked in through the large metal doors, too busy trying to keep sight of Joseph and the new boy. Heavy footsteps raced behind her.

"*Mayali run,*" Joseph said.

"*Don't talk. The Brother's will hear you.*"

"They're behind you. Run!"

"I can't run. My ankle."

The stalls were laid out in rectangular blocks, each with its own roof. The corridors crossed like tiny streets and the roof of the market high above stood like a rusty metal sky. People were walking everywhere, some pushing carts or shouldering boxes. More boxes and barrels were at the edges of the corridors as sellers stocked their shelves for the day through their side doors. Mayali found herself sidestepping or tripping over the obstructions.

"Hey, come here," the new boy said to her left. He was just visible from behind a display of jeans. She crawled through to find a space between two stalls. The boy slid aside and she moved as well as she could, given the pain. Around her, she felt the buzz of the Brothers talking to each other. When the boy tried to get her to step out, she refused.

Joseph was staying silent which meant that the Brothers would have no way to hear them. They needed to talk to each other though and as soon so Mayali felt the Brothers moving away, she held the boy's hand and they left. They navigated through the market staying low and doubling back whenever the buzz of the Brothers got too great. The boy seemed frustrated by her occasional refusals to follow him, but after a couple of close calls, he stuck to finding the most silent, obscure paths.

Around one corner they came upon Joseph at a footwear stall. He was sorting through running shoes to the side where the vendor could not see him. Joseph smiled and waved them over. He pointed to Mayali and the shoes, picked up two pairs, and slipped to a more hidden corner to try them on. Mayali knew he wanted her to use Jamesy's money to pay for the shoes, but she could feel the rising buzz of the Brothers approaching and left to join Joseph. They put their shoes on quickly, finding the fit a little big. When they were done the new boy rose, leading them through the market.

She followed his twisting path, Joseph at her side, helping her walk. They passed stalls of jewellery, clothes, bleeding meat and fragrant vegetables until they were out on the street, still moving as fast as they could. The city was packed with more people than Mayali had ever seen in one place, dodging each other as well as water-filled potholes in the streets. Loud minibuses, taxi drivers, scooters and even horse carts inched along the narrow street. Vendors lined the sidewalks and the clamor of conversation was all around.

Ahead, a uniformed policeman reached out of the crowd and grabbed the back of the new boy's shirt. Joseph and Mayali stopped too.

The policeman was average height and had a mouth overloaded with teeth. "A-ha," he said. "Rafeek, the market prince. Why you look so suspicious? Who you thief from?"

"I ain't no thief, Dracula."

The policeman twisted the boy around and patted him down.

"Nothing on you. You drop it somewhere?" he said, his disappointment at finding nothing showing. The policeman noticed Mayali and Joseph. "Or one of you got it then?" He tapped Joseph's chest with finger. "That true buck man? You got the money?"

Joseph froze, unable to reply. "He dumb. He can't talk," Mayali said.

The policeman laughed. "You buck and you dumb? Man, you must be really stupid."

Even in Mabaruma, Mayali had heard that insult used by outsiders against Amerindians. The buzz of the Brothers coming up behind them and the infuriating obstacle of the policeman's bigotry snapped Mayali's patience. She shoved him. Rafeek slipped his foot behind the policeman's ankle. Dracula tripped backward, snagged his other foot in a flooded pothole and splattered a pile of wet horse dung as he landed on his back.

The three fugitives set off again, Mayali hobbling as fast as she could, her ankle sending shockwaves of pain with every movement.

Two buildings from the market, Rafeek spun them into the front of a food shop and through a side door. Dracula shouted at them as they left his sight. They let the boy lead down the street, up a stairway to a bar playing loud dancehall music and then down into yet another street. Dracula would be searching for them in the wrong place and they were back at the market.

It was the largest building Mayali had ever seen, metallic gray with faded red roofs and small towers at the sides. A giant clock, showing the wrong time, stood above the main entrance. Rafeek walked straight under it and they followed. He led them inside a tin sheet cubicle with a ladder leading to the rafters. They climbed up and sideways, the people below never looking up. Soon they were in the clock tower itself, on a large platform above the machinery. They sat close together near the centre, because they did not want anyone to see them from the ground.

"Thanks for helping we out," Mayali said. "I don't know why you do it, but thanks."

"Yeah, well when I see the two of you jump off the boat, I figure you had to be running away with some big money. That is a North-West boat. Lot of gold in North-West. If you really want to thank me, you can give me some."

Mayali and Joseph looked at each other. "We don't have any money," she said.

"I ain't making joke, girl. You can't lie to me. People won't chase you if you didn't had something for them. I can go call them back you know."

"We not lying."

Rafeek held her gaze for a full ten seconds. "Well, damn," he said biting his lip.

As the boy leaned back against a pillar, she realized how dirty he was. His hair and face were tinged with a whitish yellow that was probably dirt. His neck was thin and taut and so were his forearms and legs. His sandals' soles were worn and cracked. Mostly though, Mayali caught a stink off him that clung to the boy like another layer of clothing.

She looked away, embarrassed. Outside, Georgetown lay revealed. Across the daily disorder of the parking lot, a large stone building relaxed behind a high iron grilled fence. It was wide, with a dome in the middle and orange walls. Despite the few vagrants camped on folded cardboard cartons outside the fence, it had an air of dignity about it.

"That is where the President live?" Mayali asked, impressed.

"Nah, that is Parliament."

"What is Parliament?"

"Just another part of the government that don't work. They got good food though. The kitchen lady used to give me leftovers there til Dracula complain to she boss."

"We got to talk to the President."

"I want to talk to he too," said Rafeek sarcastically. "I want he make me Minister of Finance."

Mayali ignored him and inspected the rest of the view. Every building seemed taller than anything she had ever imagined. They went on in the distance seemingly forever. Not far away, a bulky white concrete building stood out. Mayali assumed it was a massive church of some kind. She marvelled at a round white building close to where the river met the ocean. It was about a mile away but she could still see it clearly. She could never find her father in all this.

Joseph was standing, looking out at the city too, his expression almost panicked, but he was not saying anything.

Mayali said to Rafeek, "How long we got to stay here?" Malayi asked Rafeek.

"I don't know. Is your people. How they does behave?"

"Mostly they does just beat people 'til somebody talk. Or else they does start in the middle of where they see you last and circle out."

"Well, we better move. We can go to my house for now. After that, the two of you got to find you own way."

"This not where you live?"

Rafeek laughed. "Nah, they got a lady name Mrs. Sobers does let me sleep at the side of she house as long as I chase out all them beggar and junkie."

Mayali tried to rely on Joseph as little as possible when they got to the street, afraid of being noticed, but her ankle hurt from their exertions. She had to lean on him more than she was comfortable with. He was still not sending any thoughts and was constantly looking around.

On the ground, the city had little of the charm Mayali had felt seeing it from above. The noise from traffic was overwhelming as were the voices shouting or chattering all around. Mayali could not master the skill of walking between people as they moved through the crowd of shoppers doing business right on the sidewalk. Being attached to Joseph made it harder still. All around were rank and unpleasant smells, mostly coming from the dark thick liquid of the roadside gutters, some from the vine and bush infested spaces between many of the buildings, the rest from the piles of garbage accumulating at random crevices.

Rafeek's house was at an intersection that seemed to encapsulate the flux of the city. A clattering of unpainted huts leaned on each other in the tight space behind a gas station. Across the street was a huge brick of a building that had once been a cinema, according to Rafeek, but was now a church. A Toyota dealership was on the third corner in a wide, flat building and on the fourth was a row of two-storey, wood and concrete houses.

They entered the wood and wire-mesh gate of the third house, Rafeek giving Mayali an exaggerated 'keep quiet' sign. He started to do the same to Joseph then stopped himself. There were about two yards of space between the side of the house and the wire fence running down the sideline. Near the back was a bench and desk. Rafeek led them there, inviting them to sit. Mayali felt relief in taking the weight off her ankle.

"So you don't have any family?" she asked softly, looking at the desk she was sitting on. There was a plate with a bend at one edge, a chipped enamel cup with a painted lily design and the biggest spoon Mayali could imagine a person eating using to eat. In a cardboard box were some scraps of cloth, paper and glue and other junk that Mayali did not recognize.

"Me mother dead long time now," Rafeek said, almost mumbling, staring at a point between his heels. "I end up at the orphanage them religious people got out in Kitty. They give me the name 'Rafeek'. But I couldn't stay in that place. Too much ordering around, plus beat if you don't do what they tell you and I just didn't able with it no more."

Mayali noted he made no mention of a father. "But out here can't be better?" she asked.

"I don't know. I can't go back in any case. I too rude for them." Rafeek smiled. "I gon' stay out here and be a Rasta."

"*I have to pee,*" Joseph said.

"Joseph got to pee."

"Well, he damn well can't do it here," said Rafeek. "The lady upstairs does get vex for any little thing."

The walked to the corner where the church stood, its outside pillars creating spaces to stand half out of the street.

"*I can't do it here!*" Joseph said. "*This is a church.*"

In the end, the need overcame him and he unzipped and sprayed the wall. Rafeek joined him gleefully. An older man in a long sleeved shirt sucked his teeth at them as he passed, but everyone else acted like they didn't see.

"We can't go back to the market," Rafeek said, "so let we check out the Gardens and pick up some money for food. I got fo' stay far from Dracula for today in any case."

"How you going to get money?" asked Mayali.

"Beg. A lot of men take them girlfriend there. They don't want me spoiling the mood, so some of them pay up quick." Rafeek looked over at Joseph. "He dumb for real?"

"Yes, why you ask?"

"Me friend Goose does pretend he can't talk when he beg. He got a sign and everything. He make good money. I can't do it that way though. I like talk too much."

Mayali did not disagree.

Rafeek disappeared for five minutes near the start of their trek and returned with crutches he said he had gotten from a friend. Mayali suspected he had stolen them, but was grateful and made sure to tell Rafeek so. The boy smiled.

"What's a Rasta?" Mayali asked Rafeek when they started walking.

"People who like to smoke ganja and pretend God ordered them to do it," Joseph said.

"Rasta is consciousness," Rafeek said.

"What you mean?"

Rafeek looked sheepish. "Well, fo' tell you the truth, I don't really know. But I hear the dread them pon the corner does say so."

"Wait, what's a dread now?"

"Well, that's a rastaman. He wear he hair long, in dreadlocks and he clothes in ice, gold and green."

"Oh Lord," said Joseph. *"It's 'ites, gold and green.' Even I know that."*

They walked down Regent Street for about an hour, while Rafeek explained his understanding of Rastafari, city politics, geographical trivia and whatever caught Mayali's eye. Mayali was fascinated by the commerce and random flow of people. Everyone seemed to be buying or selling something. Some were yelling from their buses for passengers, or from their stalls to customers. A car got in the way of a motorcycle and the rider honked his horn and yelled, "Must drive pon a Sunday!"

The activity petered off into quiet as they moved east where they passed the silent bulk of the Bourda Cricket Ground and came to the end of the road.

The Botanical Gardens were a large park with a road running through its shade and quiet. Lovers used it by day, families in the afternoons, and robbers, addicts and rapists by night or so its reputation held. The iron main-gate was large and old and made the place seem important. Rafeek set up his operation just outside the gate, telling Mayali to wait inside with Joseph.

Mayali could see him approach pedestrians or cars stopped at the traffic light. She could not hear what Rafeek said, but he seemed to get money only on occasion. She hobbled up to the boy when the traffic light was red.

"Let me help," she told Rafeek. The driver of the nearest car was a thin, small man. She stuck her head through the window. "Hey. I need money. Give me some of what you got."

The man smiled once he got over his shock. "You mad? I ain't stupid. You just want money for drugs. And why you don't go bathe? You stink."

The car drove off and Mayali sniffed at her shoulder. Rafeek was laughing. She walked off as fast as the crutches allowed to the shade of a tree in the Gardens. After ten minutes Rafeek joined her with Joseph, carrying three boxes of curry and rice from one of the food vendors, as well as a large bottle of orange juice.

"Don't get vex," Rafeek said, giving her a box, "I get the food money long time. I did just seeing what extra I could pick up."

Mayali dug into the food, eating with her fingers. "I hungry. I don't got time for you to get extra. I need to find my father."

"Your father got money?"

Mayali almost smiled. Rafeek was helping them because he still hoped to get paid somehow. She tried to encourage him without actually lying. "I don't know. Probably. He smart and he does work hard."

"Which part he live?"

"I don't know. I just know he in Guyana somewhere."

"Oh, we can find him easy then," said Rafeek. At first Mayali thought he was mocking her, but he continued, "I know a obeah lady in Prashad Nagar. She does find people wedding ring and so when them lost."

"We can't go near any obeah," said Joseph. *"Obeah is a sin."*

"Alright. How we get there?" Mayali asked Rafeek.

Rafeek handed her the unopened bottle of juice. "Here. We gon' have to share. Is more cheap to buy the big bottle."

Mayali drank what she felt was her share. She watched Joseph take what was definitely more than his share as he guzzled the bottle. If Rafeek was angry at being left with less, it did not show. He took a few sips. "We can walk there easy. Is on the other side of the Gardens."

"Let we go then." Mayali handed the box to Joseph and started down the roadside on her crutches.

CHAPTER 7
Lying and Stealing

'm not going," Joseph said, looking about with a vague sense that he should find a way to stop Mayali.

"You can stay here and get tortured then," the girl said without looking back.

It was not fair how she treated him. Now that she had the crutches, Joseph had no influence over her and he wondered for the twentieth time that morning why he didn't just leave.

Well, besides the torture he would face if the Brothers caught him.

But Father Garcia had been clear that dealings with demons were always a fast route to hell. Joseph watched Mayali and Rafeek walking further and further away under the tall palms that lined the road. They disappeared around a bend and he was alone.

The park was quiet, probably because of the threat of rain Joseph guessed. A few people sat in a bandstand nearby. Others were bent over at the edge of a large pond.

Joseph wandered over to the pond and realized that the people at the water's edge were feeding manatees. There was long cut grass around the edge that had been left for visitors. The manatees were round brown bulks whose backs made islands in the water. They stuck their mouths up at the edge of the water to grab the grass scattered there, sometimes even taking the grass from the hands of the person feeding them.

With his own handful of grass, Joseph knelt at the edge of the murky water, watching a manatee back drift in towards him. He had seen many manatees on the river back home of course, but always in the distance and they always hid when they heard people. Joseph wondered if he could get this close to a wild one after he went home. The manatee he was waiting for edged closed, but a different one broke the water under his outstretched hand, emitting a gasp-like breath and spraying Joseph with water. By the time Joseph recoiled and turned back to the water, the manatee had taken his grass and disappeared. He laughed along with the two boys next to him. He sought out some more grass and offered it. This time he saw the manatee so there was no surprise and he watched it gently approach and take the grass. As he watched the manatee his mind turned to his parents. He had not told his parents anything in his text message, except that he was safe and on the *Lady Northcote.* He hoped they were not too distressed. If Mayali found her father, the man might be able to help Joseph and he could go home.

How far had Mayali and Rafeek gotten? If they got the obeah woman to help them and Joseph just happened to be there, it would still not be him dealing with the Devil. And even Jesus had talked to the Devil when he was tempted in the wilderness.

Joseph ran. The road out of the Gardens was long and mostly straight. He found Mayali and Rafeek easily. The street boy was yelling into the windows of parked cars, mocking the couples inside then running ahead before the embarrassed occupants could respond.

"Somebody's going to shoot him," Joseph said to Mayali. He regretted it instantly. The pain of using the Spider's Touch seemed more intense than ever.

"Are you okay," Mayali asked, watching his face.

"Don't Spider Talk me. It hurts."

They walked in silence. Silent for Joseph at any rate. He could see Rafeek's mouth moving constantly. Sometimes Mayali would laugh. Joseph could not remember ever seeing her laugh before.

They emerged on Sheriff Street, a major city road, and the fast traffic seemed to intimidate Mayali who stayed as far to the side as she could. She seemed even more scared crossing the street, even with the aid of a stoplight. She moved along much more happily on her crutches once they were on the narrow side streets. Prashad Nagar was a low-traffic neighborhood of middle class houses with well-painted concrete fences and relatively clean drains.

"What're all those flags?" she asked. Many of the front yards had clusters of bamboo poles with coloured triangles of cloth flying at the top.

"Jhandi flags," said Rafeek. "Hindu people does put one up whenever they do a big prayer." Not all of the houses had flags. Some of the houses had only a few flags. A few had over a dozen, tattered to various degrees to tell how long ago each had been planted.

Rafeek ignored the 'Beware of Dog' sign on the gate of one of these houses and walked right up to ring the door bell. The woman who answered a few minutes later was thin, wearing a long red sari with looping gold threaded designs. Her hair was puffy and her eyes lined with dark makeup.

"You! You thiefing lil rat!" the woman grabbed at Rafeek but he dodged.

"Miss Rhonda, listen," he said, "I bring some people—"

"Get out." Rhonda picked up an akia stick from the doorway and lifted it high.

"They need you do a work for them. The girl need to talk to her father."

Miss Rhonda stopped mid-strike and turned to Mayali. "You have money? I don't work for free."

Rafeek said, "If you tell she 'bout she father, she can get nuff money."

"I got money," Mayali said.

Joseph wondered if he or Rafeek was more surprised at this.

"Where you get money?"

"I didn't pay for the shoes," Mayali confessed.

"You can't give this devil woman that money," Joseph said, the pain lancing in his head from the Spider Talk.

Miss Rhonda did not name a price. Rather she took the whole wad of cash from Mayali with a smile. "Money not enough. I got to get a cock too."

"A what?" Mayali asked, looking amazed at the vulgarity.

"Obeah need blood. It don't matter if is a rat or a cow, but if you going to talk to jumbie they only respect male blood." There was an intense and sincere expression on Miss Rhonda's face. "So a hen won't do. I need a rooster. A need a cock."

Joseph turned away to keep from laughing.

"What wrong with woman blood?" Mayali asked, scowling.

"Woman not pure. Since Adam and Eve, Ram and Sita, and Aphrodite and Hephaestus, woman blood too weak. They mind not strong."

"But you is a woman. Your—"

Rafeek stepped in front of Mayali. "You don't have a chicken we can use?"

"A cock," corrected Miss Rhonda. "You not even pay me enough here for what you want me do. You got to bring you own damn cock. Come back when you get one." She shut the door without giving back their money.

As they filed out onto the street, Joseph felt relief that they were abandoning the obeah plan.

"You had money this whole time and had me begging?" Rafeek asked.

"But you does beg all the time."

"You think I like that? Putting out me hand in people face whole day? Making up me voice like some lil child?" The boy sucked his teeth and pulled ahead, but Mayali blocked him with a crutch in his way.

"Look, I sorry. I should have tell you."

Had Mayali ever apologized before, Joseph wondered.

It worked on Rafeek. "Alright. Don't lie to me again. Let we go find this chicken."

"Cock," Mayali said. They both laughed.

Next to Prashad Nagar, across several canal bridges, was the much less respectable neighborhood of Sophia. Its poverty was clear to Joseph, with rusty tin roofs and piles of garbage everywhere, some burnt, some rotting. Many of the yards had not just grass and trees, but bushes.

And animals were everywhere.

"I see chickens," said Mayali, "but we don't have money to pay."

"Not everything you got to pay for."

"No!" said Joseph. *"We can't steal again. We already stole shoes. We can't steal people's food."*

"It safe to thief from this place?" asked Mayali, looking at the food vendors and cigarette smokers at the corner.

"Not everything you got to thief either," said Rafeek mysteriously.

Soon, he found a yard he liked the look of and told them to wait at the gate. There was an elderly woman sitting on the front stairs of the small two-storey house. Rafeek, approached and spoke quietly, looking up at her. Within ten minutes Rafeek had caught a rooster in the yard and was closing the gate behind him, with a half loaf of bread in the bargain. The old lady waved to them as they left. Joseph waved back, while Mayali ripped open the plastic bag to get at the bread.

"That lady just give you the chicken?" she asked as she chewed and limped at the same time. "What you tell she?"

"The truth. I does thief, but I don't lie. Well, except to police, but they don't want hear truth anyway. Anyway, the lady feel sorry for we."

"But she so poor."

"Poor people can be nice too."

Joseph reached for some bread. Mayali instinctively tried to protect it then let him have it.

"Is strange how you can just walk up to somebody without knowing them and get them to give you thing."

"Not so strange," said Rafeek, smiling as he revealed his trick. "If you check she fence, it got three black mark somebody scratch. That is a beggar sign to tell who does help people."

~ ~ ~ : : ~ : ~ : ~ : : ~ ~ ~

Miss Rhonda sat them at a table in a room whose walls had been covered in black cloth. The only light came from nine candles that stood in a line behind her. Incense burned on the opposite wall, next to where the three teens sat. The scent was making Joseph panic since it reminded him of church.

Miss Rhonda took the chicken into the back and after a while returned with a dutch bottle, a clay jar large enough to need two hands. With a barking scream, she shoved the jar into the air with both hands, the sudden motion spilling blood out of the lips and down her wrists. There followed a babble of noises that sounded like baby talk mixed with the stylings of a preacher. Miss Rhonda shook her head around rapidly, her hair fluffing out even more, some coming loose from her hairpins and jutting out in long, wild bunches.

She lowered the jar to the table. Blood had run down her wrist to her elbow and she stuck out the longest tongue Joseph had ever seen and with an angled neck licked both forearms clean. After a last lick of her lips, she swallowed with a sigh of contentment.

A pack of cards appeared on the table, seemingly out of nowhere. Miss Rhonda spread them out in a jumble on the table, her hands moving slow, but precisely. Joseph's rising enthusiasm was replaced by dismay, however, once Miss Rhonda detached a metal crucifix from her necklace. It was large enough that she could dip the lower part into the blood jar and then she sprinkled blood over the top of the cards, while chanting what sounded distressingly to Joseph like the Lord's Prayer.

Miss Rhonda shuffled the cards and offered them to Mayali. "You must cut the card so they gon' show you what you want."

Mayali did as she was told. As Miss Rhonda took back the cut cards, her elbow grazed the blood jar and she snatched it to prevent a spill. Joseph's trained eyes saw her other hand slip three cards under the bottom of the card deck.

"She's cheating," he said, then told Mayali what he saw.

"Wait, let's see what she does," Mayali said. *"Maybe that's part of the obeah."*

"Of course it's part of the obeah. Obeah is the Devil's work and the Devil has to cheat."

"Be quiet."

His head was hurting again, so he had to comply.

Rhonda asked Mayali to take five cards from the top of the deck, look at them and place them back without telling her what she saw. The cards were the two, five and ten of clubs, the nine of diamonds and the Ace of Hearts.

"I need something from the person we trying to reach," Miss Rhonda said.

"Your father picture," said Rafeek.

Joseph could tell Mayali was hesitant to hand it over, but Rafeek's expectant enthusiasm seemed to guilt her into giving the ID card to the obeah woman. Miss Rhonda looked almost like she was going to dip the card in the blood, but after Mayali's body tensed the woman rested the ID on top of the playing cards. She tapped the pile three times.

"Spirit talk!" She said each time she tapped the pile. She laid the ID aside. "Them card that you touch now gon' change and the change gon' give you the message." Miss Rhonda dealt the bottom five cards out. Joseph pointed this out to Mayali, but the girl just told him to wait.

Miss Rhonda turned the first card over to reveal an Ace of Spades. "The spade is how we dig a grave. The card telling we that it speak the truth from the grave. The voice of your dead father now coming—"

"My father not dead!"

Confusion took over Miss Rhonda's face and she looked to Rafeek. "You said she want to talk to she father ghost."

"My father not dead!"

"I never tell you anything about ghost. The man alive!" Rafeek snapped.

"Well if the man alive why she need me to talk to he?"

"My father not dead!"

Rafeek said, "She got to know where to find he before she can talk to he."

By this time, Mayali and Rafeek had gotten close to Miss Rhonda who was backed up against the candle wall. This allowed Joseph to inspect the blood jar and his sense of smell pricked up. He swirled his finger around inside and waved it in front of Mayali. She and Rafeek looked at him in puzzlement for a second. He shook the jar and indicated they should smell it.

"Syrup," said Mayali, after she confirmed the smell with a taste. She grabbed the jar and whirled on Miss Rhonda. "You trying to fool we with syrup? You ain't got no shame?" Mayali threw the container against the wall like a furious prophet and it shattered. The impact knocked the candles into each other and they toppled. The black cloth caught fire instantly, and the flames shot up to the ceiling.

"Run," Rafeek shouted, pulling at Joseph.

"The picture," said Mayali.

But Rafeek shoved her out the door. Behind them the room was flooded with black smoke and they could see Miss Rhonda flapping at the fire with a towel. An entire corner of the house was on fire by the time they reached the gate. They saw Miss Rhonda run out of the back, cell phone in hand.

When the fire truck and police showed up fifteen minutes later, they left, walking west, back towards Rafeek's house. They followed the boy down his streets – Duncan, Vlissingen, Lamaha–until it felt like that had walked the entire city.

The feel of the march was grim, but Joseph held a secret joy that the obeah had failed. He tried to lighten things with a joke to Mayali. *"Well, you burnt up a ship this morning and you burn down a house this afternoon. I hope you're not going anywhere important tonight."*

The girl just gave him an annoyed look. Joseph stopped trying, but mostly because of the pain in his head.

Just after nightfall, they reached a tree-filled compound behind a medium height fence. Under the lights was a large wooden house. Guards with big guns stood at the gate. Joseph could see that it was not the kind of place that welcomed visitors to drop in and discuss Spider gods.

"That's the President house over there," Rafeek said.

"Forget that," Mayali said. "This is a disaster. We need food and all the money done."

"I know I mess up the obeah thing, but you can at least go to talk to he. You say it was important."

"You wouldn't understand. I don't got anything from my father left now. And I don't know how to find he. This place so big."

"I understand, yes. I been going to that stupid fake obeah woman every month to talk to me mother and she tell me all kind a thing about how me mother waiting for me in heaven and I must take care of meself and all kind of nonsense." Rafeek's anger came into his eyes again. "Is not you alone got problems you know."

He walked away. Joseph wasn't sure if Rafeek was abandoning them but they followed regardless. To their left was a small park behind a tall metal fence. After the first corner, the park gave way to a playground with football goals. A basketball court took up the end near them. It was surrounded by tall unkempt grass and a public toilet stood not far away. Joseph signalled that he needed to go. Before he could step inside, a shadow moved near the door and he realized a person was lying there, back against the wall.

"Stupid junkie," said Rafeek, kicking the man's legs in disgust. His victim didn't respond.

"Joseph," said Mayali.

"Yeah." His reply was brief, as the pain hit harder than ever.

"That thing the junkie is holding. The drug pipe. Rafeek has a couple in the box on his desk."

But at this point, the pain of just trying to create a reply for Mayali caused Joseph to collapse.

"Oh ra—," said Rafeek, rushing to his side. "What wrong with he?"

"I don't know. We need help."

"Woodland Hospital right back there. We can take him we self."

Every word broadcast from Mayali made Joseph's head hurt to the point of making him twitch, like light exploding in his eyes. After being carry-dragged halfway up the block, the exploding lights blurred everything. He felt time pass, but his consciousness was floating as people pulled and pushed at him.

When he was back in reality, it was morning and a doctor was staring down at his elbow. Joseph watched her fiddle with the tube stuck into the skin there, writing on her clipboard and muttering about the nurses not being careful with the IV. Mayali was sleeping in a couch nearby, her head rolled back. Rafeek was lying with his head on her lap, definitely not sleeping since his eyes were open.

"Good morning," said the doctor turning to face Joseph. She was a tall black woman with high cheekbones and large eyes. Her medium-length afro was held in place with a bandanna. And she had an enthusiastic smile. "Glad to see you awake. I'm Doctor Pinder-Hess."

"No you're not," said Joseph. For one thing, he could hear her in his head. For another, the nametag said 'Anita Pinder-Hess' but the letters seemed to swim in his mind and rearrange themselves. Mayali was up, alerted by Joseph's use of the Spider's Touch.

The doctor spoke with just her mind. *"Well, you figured that out faster than I had wanted."* She looked Mayali directly in the eye and said, *"I am Anansi the Spider."*

CHAPTER 8
THe Man with Blue Eyes

ayali sent Rafeek out to the road to buy her a drink. A doctor had strapped her injured ankle and she was supposed to keep it elevated and not walk. It also meant that Mayali, Joseph and Anansi could speak in private.

"You's a woman?" Mayali asked.

"Well, you eye working," Anansi said sarcastically.

"But in the stories you have a wife," Joseph said.

"I had a lot a wife in the last how-much-ever thousand year. You wouldn't believe how easy is that trick. You forget I had children in the story too. That one a lil harder fo' manage."

"I can't believe you real," said Mayali. The disguise was perfect. Nothing revealed that the woman in front of her was anything but human.

"You come from the land of Spider gods and you can't believe a Spider god real?" Anansi laughed.

"No, I mean, back home you like a fairy tale. They pass law saying we can't even mention you name, but we does laugh and talk about how you trick the rest of the Guatrachi and make all of them vex with you."

"How come my head doesn't hurt anymore?" Joseph asked.

"I fix you. You don't have Spider blood, but you had an injury a while back, in your brain?"

"Yes. I fell soon after I was born. It damaged my hearing. I never learned to talk."

"Well, the Spider's Touch is present under the voice of someone using it. Usually it's transmitted right into the unconscious part of the brain. But your brain is damaged and that means you hear it differently, out loud. And of course, anyone with the Touch can detect

your thoughts too. But it became painful because the channels in your brain aren't designed to communicate that way."

Mayali looked at the medical equipment in the room, some of it beeping. "And how you fix that?"

"I give he some Spider spare parts fo' —"

Joseph said, *"What? No. I can't have some demon blood in me. God will never forgive me."*

"Oh, you's one of them." Anansi flipped the folder on her chart closed. "Look, I's not actually a doctor so I got fo' leave before anybody get suspicious. I put some spending cash on the side table. Mayali, I done make sure the bill get pay and I gon' see you when he get out," she said then turned and walked away.

"If you not a doctor, then how you know how to fix Joseph?"

Anansi did not look back. *"Oh, I know many, many tricks."*

~ ~ ~ : : ~ : ~ : : ~ ~ ~

Joseph stayed in the hospital until the afternoon. The nurses seemed to understand that Mayali and Rafeek were to be given lunch along with Joseph and also that they were allowed to stay in the room at all times. Rafeek came and went, not saying where. Mayali mostly slept. After lunch the two of them were alone in the room.

"Why you're not talking to Rafeek?".

Mayali was looking out the window at the courtyard where Rafeek was in line at the cafeteria. *"That's not true."*

"You don't laugh with him anymore. You just tell him what you want to eat from the canteen."

"He's gotten moody since he found out his mother's ghost isn't really floating around watching him."

"He got moody, or you? Joseph asked. *"You've been like you're in*

mourning since you lost that picture."

"I wish you could go back to when you couldn't talk because it hurt your head."

"He saved my life," Joseph said. *"He's a good person."*

Mayali had a brief vision of Rafeek sprawled on the ground with his eyes gone all white. *"You trust people too quickly."*

"Yes, well it's a good thing for you or I wouldn't have helped you at all. Besides, you trusted him yesterday."

"Yesterday, I didn't know he was a drug addict."

"You don't know if that's true."

In the courtyard below, Rafeek held up two bottles of chocolate milk for Mayali to see and smiled, the gap in his teeth showing.

~ ~ ~ : : ~ : ~ : : ~ ~ ~

Anansi had a taxi waiting for them when Joseph was discharged. Mayali had explained to Rafeek that they had met someone who was willing to help them, but nothing more. The taxi driver said, "The boss only tell me pick up two people."

"Okay," said Mayali, keeping her eyes down.

Joseph shook his head in disagreement, letting Rafeek know he was on his side, but Mayali heard Rafeek mumble that he understood they had to leave. Joseph offered him some money. At first Rafeek waved it away, but Joseph made him take it.

The ride took them up the east coast. As Mayali felt Joseph's unspoken anger growling beside her, she said, *"Anansi said two people. I'm not going to disobey her."*

"Since when you care what anybody think? You just wanted to get rid of him."

In about twenty minutes, they arrived at a large steel building filled with heavy fabricating equipment and busy workers. There were also a lot more security guards than seemed necessary. The sign outside read, 'HSI: Hiladora Steel Incorporated'.

Anansi entered from a side door, in a gray pantsuit. "Steel is a wonderful human invention," she said. "Strong, durable and versatile. But it's still not as amazing as it could be. Spider silk, for instance, is just as strong, but much lighter. Sometimes I think—" Anansi smiled. "Well, I think a lot and not all of it is worth repeating."

They followed her past a reception desk with a large man, who looked more like a bodyguard than a receptionist, and into an air-conditioned office. In the centre were clean, white sofas. A painting of a red flamingo hung in the centre of the main wall. The top of Anansi's desk was a half circle of black metal, bare except for a computer monitor.

"Sorry about all the big English in there. I does get pompous when I in this Miss Hiladora role sometime."

Joseph ignored the humour and said, *"You could have brought Rafeek with us, you know. He's helpful and he's our friend."*

"You lucky I put you on the guest list as it is," Anansi replied. "You would be on the road with you helpful friend right now except I don't think Mayali would want leave you behind."

"Bitch," Joseph said.

"That's the truth and you better remember it."

Joseph blushed and Mayali realized that Joseph's last word had been intended as a private thought.

"How you find we in the hospital?" Mayali asked. "How you know Joseph need help?"

"I always got me eye on what the Brothers doing. When I hear about you setting fire to the *Lady Northcote,* I had a friend follow y'all. I was only planning on finding out what you doing, but once the boy collapse, I see a chance to learn more about he."

"You got spy with—"

Anansi waved her hand in dismissal, her black-painted fingernails shining. "We ain't come here fo' talk about me. I want know you story and I want to know what you planning."

Mayali told her tale, starting with her escape from Zolpash and ending with the disastrous session at Miss Rhonda's house.

"As for plan," Mayali added, "I ain't got no plan. I don't know which part me father live and I don't know anybody who could help Jalana."

"You can help us," Joseph said to Anansi.

"The real question is if I want help you."

"But you're not friends with the Brothers."

Anansi sucked her teeth. "They does behave stupid when you shake them up. I don't want play that game."

"Well, where is a good place fo' hide?" Mayali asked.

"Not Guyana. This place full of them."

"How about Brazil or Venez—"

"You know," said Anansi, standing up and stroking her jaw, "I might be able to help you with you father."

"How?"

"A man name Zarco. Everybody does call he 'The Brazilian' but he from Guyana. He does bring gold and girls and drugs in and out the country."

"He don't sound easy to meet," Mayali said.

"He don't sound like anybody we want to meet," said Joseph.

"You right. He not easy to meet. And he not a somebody you want to meet. Is probably not a good idea actually. And is only a small chance he know—"

"No," said Mayali. "We gon' talk to him. How we can meet he?"

"He does move about. I only know that he come to town every couple week fo' dog fight. He got some big project he working on in the interior."

"Dog fight?" asked Joseph.

"Yeah. He like that kind of thing. The next one is a week from now,

I think. If you go there, you could meet he."

"*They put dog to fight?*"

"Well, why not? They put people fo' fight war all the time."

~ ~ ~ : : ~ : ~ : : ~ ~ ~

They waited six days.

Anansi put them in the top flat of the Great Coastal Lodge, a small inn which she owned, next door to the Hiladora steel factory. She warned them not to leave since they might be recognized by an ally of the Brothers. While the three-storey hotel had seemed from the outside undeserving of the name 'Great', it turned out to be more luxurious than anything Mayali had ever experienced. The entire floor was air-conditioned and they each had a room for themselves. In fact, there were two extra rooms, each with its own bathroom, which Joseph said seemed wasteful. Not to mention the hot water.

A different guard came in once a day to clean and deliver food. Anansi did not visit, which frustrated Mayali. She had many questions. Anansi sent them several sets of new jeans and T-shirts, as well as socks and good running shoes. And they got new backpacks.

On the third day, she got a red and black German knife as a gift from Anansi. It was far superior to the homemade thing she had brought over from Zolpash, smaller, but with a thicker, sturdier blade. And it flipped open, so she didn't need a sheath for it. There was a built in clip at the side.

Joseph was tense the entire time, reading the newspapers for mentions of his family. He found only a note that Father Garcia was in stable condition at the Georgetown hospital and a report on a fire on-board the *Lady Northcote* that did not mention them or the Brothers.

Joseph wanted to visit the hospital, but Mayali convinced him that the Brothers were probably watching for him.

"But I'm the reason he's hurt," Joseph said. *"I should have helped him."*

"Why didn't you?"

"I saw you running. I couldn't think properly. You weren't helping him either."

"He wasn't my friend," Mayali said.

Joseph swam in the pool sometimes, but Mayali did not join him. After nearly drowning twice, she was scared of getting into water.

Mayali watched television and learned cards from Joseph, though he criticized her playing constantly. There was a system to playing cards she soon realized and while she could not match Joseph, she understood at least why she was losing. The most frustrating lesson for her was learning that sometimes the cards you were dealt were unplayable.

"Suppose the obeah woman was right and my father's really dead?" she asked Joseph. The two were in the middle of playing a card game.

"Why you worrying about that now. It was fake."

"The syrup and so, yes, but suppose she really had power? Like when people go to church they don't have to dress up to pray, but they do it to make the place feel a way they like. Well, suppose the blood and all that is just dress up and the obeah power inside her is real?"

"No, if she had the power by itself she would have just used it." Joseph won the last hand and the game with it. *"No one needs all that fancy dancing around if they can just get straight to the truth."*

"Like Father Garcia and the communion wine?"

Joseph gave her a cross look and shuffled for the next game.

Joseph also started teaching her to read. The very concept was problematic at first, but after that the main issue was the inconsistencies of the letter sounds in various words. She read the newspapers, always fearful that some bad news about Rafeek would show up, him lying dead of a drug overdose most likely.

The boy's brash mouth and weirdly gracious manner had been charming. Mayali remembered where he lived. She could go find him and she could see more of the city with him. But, in the end, Mayali decided he had to be safe. Rafeek had survived well enough on the street before she arrived after all.

~ ~ ~ : : ~ : ~ : : ~ ~ ~

On the day of the fight, a Sunday, Anansi finally appeared again. She gave them both cell phones and told them the devices were only able to call each other or her. They should take a mini-bus into Georgetown she added, then a taxi to the fight. That way no one would be able to trace them back to Anansi. She also gave them money, more money that Mayali had ever seen.

On the cramped minibus ride, which smelt of sweat and hair, they spoke silently to each other.

"Nobody said you had to come," Mayali told him.

"I want to see this dog fight."

The taxi driver gave them a curious look when they told him their destination, then requested payment in advance. The ride took them alongside the edge of the Botanical Gardens and again Mayali wondered about Rafeek. She turned away. On the other side of the road a tower rose in the distance, alongside a giant satellite dish.

"That's the National Radio Station," Joseph told her when she asked about it.

"National? Like the whole country?"

"Well, most of it. It doesn't reach North-West or other places far away, but they have other antennas that carry the signal up and down to all the big towns."

"So most of the people in the country listen that one radio station?"

"No. There are others, but that one reaches the most people."

Their destination was in Ruimveldt, an old textile factory that had been locked up, unused for a decade. The guards were part of the fight organization because they were checking people at the gate and letting them in. Maybe they were even the ones running it, Mayali thought. She limped over, much more steady on her feet after a week of healing.

"You can't come in here, buck girl," one of the guards said when she reached the entrance.

"Is not here is the dog fight place?" The other guards were watching her now.

"Yes. But only betting people and dog owner can come in here. You don't look like you got any money. You got a dog."

"He's me dog." She pointed at Joseph. "You want fight he?"

The guard laughed. "You mouth hot girl. But I still not letting you in."

"I want to bet." Mayali flashed a wad of cash. "I come to bet against the Brazilian."

While the guard in front looked stunned, one of those behind said, "Whooo. You better leave that one alone, Georgie. Best don't interfere with Zarco business."

There was mostly empty space in the building aside from the rusty hulks of old machines whose purpose Mayali could not decipher. Light filtered in from the windows high above the ground, all of which had cracks and holes. A square ring had been created out of chain link fencing near one corner. The fence was about five feet tall, the supports held upright by concrete blocks. Dark red stains spread out like a world map over the concrete floor.

"Where do we sit?" Joseph asked.

There were about thirty men nearby. No women. The wall near the ring had been turned into makeshift bleachers with planks laid on chunks of concrete and scrap iron and Mayali opted to go there, as out of the way as she could be.

"If you see anyone that looks like they could be the Brazilian, tell me."

That thought shrivelled when the dogs came out. The crowd had swelled by about twenty people and a man in a dress shirt and neat haircut was sitting next to Joseph. He and the rest of the men cheered as the first pair of growling, snarling dogs were brought in on chains. They were huge, as high as Mayali's waist. Their jaws bulged and curved in a way that reminded Mayali of an alligator. They both had their tails cut short and their muscles flexed under their short coats of hair.

The owners led the dogs inside to opposite sides of the pen. A bearded man in dreadlocks and a knit cap in red, green and yellow stood in the centre of the cage and addressed the crowd, "Alright, alright! First fight today. We got Fidel going to take on Tiger." Immediately, the crowd started to place bets with each other, making rude comments about the dog they bet against, even about the person they put money against.

Fidel had a black coat and was slightly bigger than Tiger who was dark brown. The dogs barked and snapped at each other from across the cage. The owners held them by their collars while the chains were removed and at the signal from the man with the dreadlocks, the dogs were let free.

Mayali had expected some circling and testing out, but the dogs flew at each other straight on, their forelegs shoving at each other as they tried to get in position for a bite. The dogs' growling was clear and loud enough to be heard above the shouts of the crowd. Their owners stood to the sides shouting as well, but did not approach. The dreadlocks man stood by like a referee. He was the referee, Mayali realized, but there did not seem to be any rules. The dogs bit at each other's legs and side and faces. It went on for at least ten minutes and Mayali would have been bored at the repetitive action if not for the constant feeling of shame and shock.

Fidel was getting the better of Tiger.

"Big dog always win," said the well-dressed man next to Joseph.

Mayali saw Joseph look at him with an expression that was hate and nausea combined. The man noticed it too.

"What wrong with you? You never see dog fight before?"

A loud squeal and whimper shot through the factory. Tiger was on his side with the big dog over him. Fidel's jaw had a firm grasp of Tiger's front leg which he held at a twisting angle as Tiger fought against the air to get up. The referee signalled the fight was over.

"Too bad," Joseph's neighbor said. "That just starting to get good. Broke foot always end a fight too easy."

"That didn't look easy at all," said Mayali.

"Like you don't like the fight or what?"

"Is cruel to do this to dog."

"No," said the man, smiling like he was educating them. "Them dog love to fight. You see how they want it when they start? Even the little one? Dog like them is fighting dog. That is they purpose in life. You can't stop a dog from doing—"

A deep voice interrupted from behind them with a grumble. "You talking sheer nonsense, Sunil." Mayali turned to see a man who had not been there a minute before. He was carrying two pounds of gold chains around his wide neck, wearing a black mesh vest on his heavy body. His beard was long and straight. Wide, blue sunshades covered his eyes completely. An intricate design of waves was tattooed on his fat, dark arms. "Them dog fight because they frighten," the man said. "They see the other dog and they mind tell them is danger and the only way they train to deal with danger is fighting."

Sunil seemed scared at getting attention from this man and said nothing.

"The thing about a dog," the big man continued, "is that they love you no matter how you treat them. So if you show them that you happy when they win a fight, then they try even more hard for win. A animal would kill for food, but if they think it would hurt them, they don't press the issue. Fear and love is the only thing ever make man or animal fight in this world."

Mayali watched as a limping Tiger was led out of the building by his owner, who yanked him along by the chain. Sunil remained silent and still beside Joseph.

"You scared Sunil?" the big man asked.

"Yes, Brazilian."

"Don't worry. We only talking. Right now I need a lil private talk with me niece and nephew here." Sunil scampered away.

Joseph said, *"Mayali, I can't take this anymore. Let's leave."*

"No. Didn't you hear? This is Zarco. The Brazilian. We have to talk to him."

Zarco put a heavy hand on each of their shoulders. "The thing about a dog, though, is that they don't naturally want to fight. You got to make them understand that fighting is how to deal with another animal. You can't do that all at once. You got to teach them one lesson at a time."

Mayali said, "I'm trying to find my father. I think that—"

"Oh no," Zarco's voice rumbled into her mind. *"Your father is a lesson for another time. I need to give you lesson number one first."*

"He's a Brother," said Joseph.

"No. He looks normal. He's not wearing a disguise or anything."

"Look at the door," Zarco told them.

A man entered dragging a brown dog. It took them a moment to recognize it.

"Daisy!" said Joseph. The dog's tongue was hanging out from thirst and his back and legs had long, shallow cuts from being beaten.

"Come with me," Zarco said, squeezing their shoulders. *"Just smile and act like I'm showing you a good time. If you try to run, my guards will catch you. Human guards, not Brothers, so you won't feel them*

coming."

The crowd parted, allowing Zarco to get them right up against the fence. Daisy whimpered as he was shoved into the cage.

CHAPTER 9
Chloe

aisy ran around the cage barking, biting at the fence and digging at the concrete before settling into a corner, trembling. The white blaze on his chest heaved up and down.

A man brought in the other dog. It seemed larger even than Fidel to Joseph, with a sleek coat that was a peculiar shade of gray that was almost blue. Its muscles bulged and slid under its skin, straining for action.

"This is my dog," said Zarco. *"Her name's Chloe. I got her as a puppy from a lawyer who failed to keep two of my men out of jail. He didn't want to give her to me, but nobody says no after you put two bullets in their knee."*

The handler brought Chloe into the cage. Joseph noticed that unlike Fidel and Tiger, Chloe kept her head still, growling almost inaudibly as she stared across at Daisy. Her body was pointed at her target, her snub of a tail doing slow tick-tocks as her back legs tensed to leap.

"Chloe has never had a real fight. She's only fifteen months old. But it's time she learned to kill. The best way for a fighting dog to learn that is with a dog weak enough to lose, but strong enough to make it angry. Daisy here is perfect."

The man in the Rasta hat put on heavy gloves and walked over to Daisy with a roll of duct tape. He grabbed the resisting dog and wrapped its snout five or six times.

"But that's not fair," Joseph said. *"Daisy can't bite back."*

Zarco chuckled. *"I don't want a fair fight. I need Chloe to stay healthy for the real fight next month. This is just to show her off, so that people will want to bet on her when the time comes."*

The dreadlocks man turned to the crowd and said, "I know this suppose to just be a show, but if you want to bet, go ahead. Nobody stopping you. We got Chloe here and the stupid dog in the corner look like he name Milkbone or something."

"He name Daisy!" said Mayali.

The crowd seemed inclined to laugh at this, but seeing her with her 'uncle', the Brazilian made them hold their thoughts.

"Alright, Daisy is the other dog," said dreadlocks man. "Remember, you can always bet on how long you think Daisy gon' last. I had a stray dog one time that put up a five-minute fight, so you never know. Let we start."

Chloe sprang at her handler's command and Daisy ran. He dodged exactly once before the bulky dog shouldered him onto the ground and bit into his throat. Daisy yelped a few high-pitched squeals, muffled by the tape, and twisted around. His small size helped him. Daisy popped loose and was on his feet running while Chloe was left looking for him.

Blood was leaking down Daisy's neck. His chest had gone pink as the blood soaked into it. He had nowhere to escape. Chloe pounced on him from behind as Daisy jumped towards the top of the cage. Joseph thought the weight of the bigger dog should have broken Daisy's back, but there was a scramble on the ground and Daisy again broke free, half his tail gone, blood dripping from the severed end. The tape was also flapping loose where Chloe had bitten into his face. Daisy was taking panting breaths through his now open mouth.

Chloe charged again. Injured or not, Daisy was quicker than Chloe and he used his speed to sidestep and bite. He connected with Chloe's head and sunk his teeth in. Whatever it was he had grasped held firm as Chloe growled and shook her neck wildly, swinging Daisy around. Chloe swung her body around, banging the much smaller dog against the fence and Daisy's mouth detached from Chloe's face in a spurt of blood. For the first time, Chloe made a sound of pain and backed away, unsteady. Her eyeball was hanging by the nerve on her cheek, blood pouring in all directions. Her vision was blocked, Joseph realized. She backed away until she hit the cage with her rump.

The referee called for the handler to attend to Chloe, but Daisy had realized his chance to survive was now. He growled at the man then bit Chloe's undefended foot. The dreadlocks man made to grab Daisy with his gloves, but the crowd yelled at him.

"Let the dog fight, Percy."

"Let Daisy put licks on she."

Percy the referee looked at Zarco, who nodded slightly. Daisy circled Chloe and bit her a few times in the back leg, drawing blood. Chloe made a few blind grabs with her jaws, but Daisy pranced around them. The small dog sensed the eyes were the key and faked left then lunged at Chloe's remaining eye when she turned her head. He nearly got there, but Chloe snapped back and got a bite into the top of Daisy's neck.

With a growl of triumph, Chloe shouldered Daisy into the fence and stunned him, exposing his throat, which she bit into with a roar. Daisy wheezed rather than squealed and then his sounds petered out into quiet whimpers as he feebly kicked his legs at Chloe.

"*Sounds like that's the end of the fight,*" said Zarco, forcing them to the corner of the cage where the dogs were, "*but the lesson isn't over yet.*"

Daisy was dying. He was on his back, his head pinned against the fence while Chloe kept her teeth clamped onto his windpipe. His eyes circled and caught sight of them and then his nose twitched. He whimpered and reached his paws up at Joseph, who touched them softly. He stroked Daisy's nose with his other hand and the dog licked his fingertips twice then closed his eyes and died.

~ ~ ~ : : ~ : ~ : : ~ ~ ~

They did not see any other fights. They were placed to sit on the floor in a long, narrow room, two large men standing inside the locked door, staring down at them from the far side. One of the guards had their phones. The other had Mayali's German knife. Joseph and Mayali could hear the distant cheering from the cage.

"Daisy died asking us to help him," Joseph said. Mayali did not reply. *"We could have let him out. Maybe we could have climbed in and—"*

The door opened and one of the dog handlers came in with Chloe, whose eye was still dangling, though the bleeding was only a trickle now. He tied the dog to an iron pipe running on the floor, not far from them, and left. Chloe seemed still disoriented by the loss of half her vision and shifted in a half circle both ways before sitting, her breathing strained.

"I should put Chloe's eye back in," said Joseph.

"That thing just killed Daisy and you want to help it? And put its eye back? It won't even let you get near. It would eat your hand."

"I want you to tell her I'm a friend."

"I don't know dog talk."

"Tell her with your mind," said Joseph. *"It can work. The same way the Brothers can trick people into thinking that they're police.* Joseph did not know if Mayali was trying to help him. He walked towards Chloe with small steps, his hands held out. The men at the door were laughing at him as he bent lower, getting closer and closer. The dog's good right eye tracked him as she stood. She growled. Joseph paused and stretched his open hand out farther, letting the dog sniff him. After the first sniff, she pulled back and took a longer inspection of him, her nose rubbing along the fingertips. She licked his palm and whined, almost like she was asking a question. With his other hand, Joseph reached behind Chloe's ears, careful to avoid a cut there as he stroked

her head.

The men at the door stopped laughing.

It took a few minutes of his touching for the dog to relax enough to sit. When she was letting him stroke her left cheek without flinching, he lifted the loose eyeball and with one smooth motion pressed it into the socket. Chloe jumped back and whimpered, but then her tail nub started wagging and she bumped her head against Joseph's hand.

"I can't believe that worked," Mayali said.

"Me neither."

Mayali moved a little closer to Joseph but seemed to still be afraid of Chloe. Joseph sat against the wall with Chloe resting her head in his lap. Mayali took a half step farther back when he unhooked Chloe's chain from her collar.

It took two hours for the fights to be over. Chloe heard the movement outside first and jumped up with a fearful whine. Joseph stood and returned to the back wall with Mayali.

Hakk, the Brother in the red robe, entered, not bothering to disguise himself from the human guards. *"Insolent Sister, you have been found and—"*

Chloe barked and Brother Hakk jumped.

"Scared of dogs?" Mayali asked.

"Yes, he is," said Joseph. *"See, he's staying at the far end."*

The guards did not seem at all mystified that the three of them were having a silent conversation.

"Your filthy beast is an abomination," said Brother Hakk. *"When the Spider gods come, all dogs shall be torn to pieces in—"*

"Wow, you people are all alike," said Joseph. *"You sound like Zarco wanting to rip animals in—"*

"I am nothing like Zarco!" The wild anger in Hakk's voice stunned Joseph. The Brother continued speaking, his face hidden, but his voice clear. *"Zarco is a petty bureaucrat whose power has corrupted him. He enjoys the pleasures of this world far too much when it is those pleasures*

the gods will destroy."

The door creaked and Zarco came in, still wearing his blue shades. Percy, the referee, stood between the other two guards.

"Go back to the plant," Zarco said to Hakk.

"I wish to stay and witness the interrogation of—"

Zarco slapped Hakk.

"Look," said Zarco, *"you may be some famous commander back in Zolpash, but I was selected by King Arrak himself to represent him here on Earth. I speak with his voice. Do as you're told."*

With a hateful glance in Joseph's direction, Brother Hakk left. Percy locked the door.

Chloe cowered as Zarco walked by. If he noticed her eye was back in place, he did not question it.

"Now, children," said Zarco, *"we're only talking in this room. Talking is easy. After we talk, I'll take you back outside where the ring is and things will either get even easier or they will get very, very hard."*

"You're lying," said Mayali. *"Anything we tell you, you're still going to kill us."*

"I didn't say I was going to let you live. I said you could have it easy or hard. Fidel is still out there and he's eager to actually kill something today. Maybe two somethings."

"We're here looking for my father, Franklyn Theodorus."

"Franklyn Theodorus is a fugitive from justice and from the gods. You're fortunate that I don't know where he is, for I would have killed him. You're also a fugitive, but the gods have sent word that you're not to be killed. Strange."

"I thought you said you weren't going to let us live?"

"Clearly, I meant the boy," said Zarco. *"The gods didn't mention him."* It was hard for Joseph to read Zarco's face without him moving his lips. Harder still given his glasses and his bushy beard. *"I'll make sure the boy doesn't suffer if you tell me how you found me."*

"I came looking for my—"

"HOW?"

"I heard from a boy on the street that you move people around. I thought you might know where my father was."

"You want to test me?" asked Zarco. *"Was lesson number one not enough? You should be more like Chloe."* The dog was still braced against the wall, head down. *"That dog, her entire life, has been scared of me. I made her scared of me, with whips and sticks and all kinds of amusing things. And because she's scared of me, she tries to make me happy."*

Joseph said, *"Well, Daisy made a joke out of all your training."*

"No," said Zarco. *"I don't raise a dog to win for me. I raise a dog to die for me. If Chloe dies now or dies in four years, it doesn't matter. My power over her is the same."*

"Power over a dog doesn't take much." Mayali said.

"You're right. People die so much more spectacularly. I think it's time for lesson number two." Zarco grabbed Joseph by the shirt and yanked him toward the door.

"Chloe. Chloe, stop him!" Mayali yelled.

"Chloe?" Zarco said. *"She can't even look me in my face. She's not—"*

Chloe jumped high, biting into the tall man's shoulders. Her weight was enough to send him into the wall and then to the ground, where he coughed as he clutched his shoulder. Chloe turned to pounce on Zarco, but he was already gaining his feet and Mayali told Chloe to run. Percy was out the door immediately while the other two guards just watched – the sight of a crazy-eyed dog charging them with its massive teeth bared had paralyzed their feet. Joseph knew that would not last and made Chloe keep running. She snapped at a guard, causing him to drop one of their phones. Joseph swooped, grabbed it and kept on running.

Ahead of them, Percy was nearly at the exit. Before he reached the door, Chloe made the distance and leaped onto his arm, swinging him down and around. Percy landed on his back. The dog made for a killing strike at his throat, but Joseph grabbed her collar and kept running, noticing on the way out that Percy had wet his pants.

Through Mayali's mind, Joseph heard her say to the man on the ground, "I got a Rasta friend. He tell me Rasta don't support cruelty. You is not no Rasta."

Despite Mayali's slight limp, they ran out of the gate before the surprised guard there could react and Joseph gave Mayali the phone. She dialed as they ran.

"We need help," Mayali was shouting into the phone. "We need help now." Though she let Joseph track the conversation through her mind, he couldn't hear the person on the other end of the call. "I don't know which way is West," Mayali snapped. She listened for a while and said, "Yes, I see it. Good."

'It' was a yellow car, speeding towards them. When it braked at their toes, Joseph saw that Anansi was driving. She was wearing a T-shirt and jeans with her hair braided and under a cap. She did not wait for the doors to close behind them before speeding off and dodging down the potholed side streets of Albouystown.

CHAPTER 10
The Spider Queen

nansi's home was an apartment in the rear of the Hiladora steel factory, if apartment was a word that applied to such a bizarre structure. Entry was via an elevator into the centre of the room. At the front was an oval, floor-to-ceiling window toward the sea. Near the horizon, Mayali saw the back end of a ship, its front obscured as it sailed seaward into the mist of a rainstorm. Soon, the ship was swallowed up and the rain lumbered toward the shore.

The window had no glass and no railing, so Mayali stayed away from the edge, near the sofas set around a circular rug in the centre of the dark floor. Joseph walked at the lip of the window, looking over the side as though there was no two-storey drop there. Chloe seemed nervous about the height, but she stayed at Joseph's heel. The high ceiling was held up by giant steel rafters, seemingly placed in random directions and connected to steel pillars at the sides. The room, painted a textured brown, narrowed towards the back, the steel supports getting closer and closer to each other until they seemed to jumble at the end of a long tunnel.

Anansi was in there now, in whatever room was behind the mess. She had changed cars at a car wash in Bourda, then driven to Water Street and put them in a garbage truck before bringing them here. Joseph sat with Chloe the entire way and Mayali kept silent waiting until Anansi had gotten them far from Zarco before asking any questions.

Now Anansi came back out, her hair loose and free, wearing a dark red dress with thin, black stripes, and high heels.

"You know that Zarco was a Brother. Why you send us in there?" Mayali demanded as soon as Anansi stepped in.

"He's a Brother?" Anansi looked over at Joseph. "Really?"

"You say how you got spies on the Brother side," Mayali snapped. "How you don't know Zarco is the boss?"

"I know he was running things, but I thought he was a regular man getting order from the real boss. You sure he's a Brother? I look at him real close. He don't look like no Brother underneath. With a Brother, you can see under they trick. See how they really look."

"He spoke to us in the Spider Talk," Joseph said.

"So?" asked Anansi, sitting on a sofa. *"You can talk like that."*

"Yes, but I'm special, remember?" Joseph was near a wall to the side where a counter, cupboard and stove sat. He removed some Cheerios and gave it to Chloe in a bowl with milk.

Anansi did not seem to care about the dog eating her food. "Zarco must be have some better trick then. Like the way I can do it. When I leave Zolpash, I destroy my work, but they must be figure it out by now."

"What work?" Joseph asked.

"I was like a scientist, but for magic. I find a way to ... well, I find a way to do plenty thing, but one thing was to make a Spider take a shape like people."

"So that isn't an illusion, like with the Brothers? You really have a woman's body?"

"Yes. Right now I could give birth to perfectly normal human children if I wanted. I done it before." Anansi smiled. "And if any other Spider want to come over here to Earth, they got to be able to do this. Otherwise, no magic can't hide them. People would see them too quick. That's why all the other Spider stay back in Zolpash and the Brother them run things over here."

"That man nearly kill we," Mayali said.

"Yes, well I couldn't tell you nothing about your father, so I figure I could at least use you to shake up Zarco. And it work. Now I know he's a Brother."

"We did already get away from them pon the boat," said Mayali.

"They didn't know where we went. We was safe."

"Don't fool yourself. You wasn't never safe from them in this town. They would have find you anyway."

"Life has value," said Joseph. *"You can't play with people like that."*

"I been playing with people since before Jesus born," Anansi said, pouring herself a glass of water from a jug on the table. "The people I leave behind want to come here and take over. I can't be polite when I trying fo' stop them."

"Why you leave?" Mayali asked, finally sitting and taking water herself. Even after six months on Earth it still seemed like a wonder to see the clear liquid flowing. It tasted so much better than powdered hardwater too. "The story say you thief from the rest of the Guatrachi."

"I thief a lot of thing, yes," said Anansi, smiling. Then she got an edge of anger in her voice. "But that's not why I leave. They didn't like how I was making things over there and finding out how things work. I leave so I could be a real Spider, so I could build things."

"Spider does break things down. They don't build nothing they own self," Mayali responded.

Anansi laughed. "What you know about Spider?"

"We all learn the story when we was children." Mayali switched to her mind voice. *"Turtles were the first Lords of creation who put the stars, moons and planets in their places. The Serpents ruled Zolpash. Then the Spiders came from inside the Earth and went to war with the Serpents for they claimed that the land was theirs and only the sky belonged to the serpents."* Mayali could see that Joseph wanted to say something about how Serpents and Spiders could not be real, but when you were sitting in Anansi's living room, with your dog eating her cereal, it was hard to deny her existence. Mayali continued her story. *"The Spiders destroyed the Serpents, leaving nothing but their skins behind, scattered over the land."*

"That is mostly lie," said Anansi. "You ever hear about Arachne?"

"Who?"

With the intonation of a storyteller, Anansi spoke: "A couple thousand years gone, in the time when the god Zeus and he mighty family rule Greece, a shepherd daughter name Arachne study how to weave at the foot of the goddess Athena. The goddess used to teach the ordinary people different craft during the time when there wasn't no war. Arachne get even better at weaving after she return home. Just seeing she weave was a wonder, as she hand flicker and play pon the loom with the wool, creating picture and pattern full with detail.

"The nymph them love to watch Arachne weave and eventually they tell she that she must be almost as good as Athena. But Arachne get offended and say how she was actually a greater weaver than Athena even. Eventually, Athena self hear about this boasting and she come visit Arachne, disguising sheself as a old woman. Athena tell Arachne that she should apologize for insulting the goddess. Arachne reply say that she only talk the truth and that if the goddess didn't like it, Athena had to prove that she better.

"Right then Athena throw back she cloak and accept the challenge. Each one of them weave four scene, Athena showing times when the gods did punish people for they pride and Arachne showing the gods them abusing humans.

"Athena get so vex! Not only from Arachne showing bad things about the god them, but she could see clear that Arachne was really better at weaving than she. Athena destroy the loom! And everything Arachne weave too. Then the goddess strike Arachne right in the forehead with she spear and curse the girl and all she pickney – that them must weave forever, with never no rest. And that's how Arachne become the first Spider on Earth."

"Wait, that can't be right," said Mayali. "There ain't got no Spider name Arachne."

"And no goddess named Athena," added Joseph. *"Those are all myths."*

"A lot of it is just story," Anansi admitted, "like the part about

Athena throwing off she cloak and so. But the truth there underneath. Arachne was a real girl and Athena was a real goddess and Athena turn Arachne into a monster for being a sinner."

Mayali said, "It shouldn't be a sin to do something better than other people. Is not fair to punish she."

"No god ever deal fair with nobody in this life, Mayali. You should remember that. But the story didn't over there." Anansi seemed eager to tell the rest, like she hadn't spun a good tale in a while. "Even though she was the first Spider of Earth, Arachne was only a mockery of the real Spider them who ruled what we now calling Zolpash. Arachne hide sheself in the dark passage them of the land and come to find she way to Zolpash, she heart burning for revenge pon Zeus and he people and the whole Earth on top.

"The Spiders them in Zolpash, they was creators, you see, powerful beings. The Turtle them was they worker and the Serpent them they put fo' be guardians over their creation. The rockslider, they was the people of the land and no human didn't live there. Not yet.

"Arachne set sheself in-between the true Spider them, first as a refugee, then as they student and last as a parasite. She tell lie and talk name, setting one side against another, 'til the power of the Spider god them burn out in murder and backstabbing. After she kill out the first Spider them, Arachne set she self up as queen over them children, keeping them weak so that none of them would challenge she. She give them false history. She tell them that they conquer the land in the war with the Serpent. But the truth was really that all the Serpent rebel against Arachne fo' protect the true Spider them against she mischief. Arachne make she people ignorant about them own past. So they didn't know they was creators, so that they wouldn't find back the godly power inside they self. And is so how she rule them up to this day."

"Now I know you talking nonsense," said Mayali. "There ain't got no Spider queen. Is King Arrak who in charge. He—"

Anansi laughed and Mayali realized the truth.

Joseph asked, *"So, Arrak is really Arachne, and the king is really a queen? Why's she trying to fool the other Spiders?"*

"Is not them she fooling," said Anansi. "In fact, all them Spiders that call they self 'Lord' and who say that female blood dirty and woman must stay away from real water and all that? All of them 'Lord' is female. There got male Spider wandering around Zolpash, but they weak and they does stay out of the way."

"But if they's women," asked Mayali, "why they set up their whole world against women?"

Anansi said, "Because lying is how Arachne know to make thing now. After she start to carry over people from Earth to Zolpash, she realize that she could never kidnap enough to do the work she want. She had to breed them over there too. So after a while, she take the women out of the work and put them fo' make children. A setup like that can't work unless the men in charge. And you can't tell people the men must be in charge if all the Spider is woman."

Mayali nodded her understanding. "So she make another lie."

Joseph left the kitchen with Chloe at his side and sat on the carpet. The dog sat, looking alert and giving Anansi an extra dose of suspicion.

"You gon' need to take that thing to a vet," Anansi said. "That eye gon' get infect otherwise."

Joseph nodded.

"I know a good one," Anansi said. "I gon' let her come around tomorrow."

Joseph nodded again.

"You won't need to pay or anything. I gon' handle that."

"What happened to Athena?" Joseph asked. *"None of those Greek gods are around now."*

"They might be. All god does just kind of fade away eventually. People forget about them and they lose they power."

"So what're you saying?" asked Joseph. *"That gods don't create*

people, people create gods?"

Anansi sighed and then smiled. "I been trying to find that out for a long time. What I know for sure is that the more people believe in any god, the more strong that god end up being."

"That's why you come here," said Mayali. "Ain't it? You want set yourself up as a god over here. Trying to get power."

Anansi smiled and examined her manicured nails for a moment. "Since I come over, I live everywhere in this world, from Jamaica to Japan, and everywhere I go I make sure I give them a Spider-god story. I even find a chap in New York to make me into a superhero." Then Anansi added, "I need power to fight back against Arachne. This world not safe from she and she want break it into pieces. I think if she could eat this world, she would do it."

"You know a lot about her," said Joseph.

"Well, yeah. I was she most trusted and loyal servant." Anansi shrugged. "At least I make her think so for a while. "

"All this story don't make no difference to me. I don't care about this world," said Mayali. "I want find my father. You lie last time. This time, tell we the truth."

"The truth?" asked Anansi. "The truth is you father probably dead. Them Brother don't mess around. They track down people when they escape Zolpash. And they don't let them live."

Her father had promised to return for her. Five years ago, he had told her that he would be back. All the risks she had taken since her mother died, all the bargains she had made and all the pain she had suffered were only to find the man she remembered from her childhood. She wanted to hold him and see him smile and hear him say her name. And yes, somewhere in the bottom of the reward pile, she wanted to hear him explain why he had not come back.

He had promised.

Joseph put an arm around her, but said nothing.

She hated the fact that he would do that, that he would feel sorry for her. Mayali wiped her eyes and shook her head at Anansi, "He not dead. You think you know 'bout things, but you ain't know me father." She laughed, a little too loud. "He here and I gon' find he. If not now, later. But if I don't got no father to find right now, then is time I keep me promise and get serious about meeting the President." She shook off Joseph's arm and said to him, *"The house he live in look too hard to get in, but he can't be in there all the time. We can find he outside at some function and talk to he there."*

"We'll need proof," Joseph said. *"Important people won't believe things without proof."*

"It not gon' do you any good," Anansi said.

"Why not?" Mayali gave Anansi a harsh stare, upset that Anansi seemed not to want her to do anything.

Anansi stayed calm. "What make you think he don't know already?"

"If he know," Mayali said, "he would have do something about all the Spider."

"That is if he able to do anything. That is if he want to do anything in the first place."

"Why he wouldn't do nothing? He's the President. He—"

"A place like this, you don't know how far corruption go. Suppose he work for them? Suppose you go to meet him and he arrest you and send you back to Zolpash? You at least got to be sure."

"So we can't trust nobody?" Mayali said.

"No. Trust no one. Not even me." Anansi stood. "Is time fo you go back to you room. I will see you in the morning."

Leaving Anansi's building, Joseph patted Chloe's head as though he was deep in thought. *"We should just leave. She doesn't care about us. We need to find a way to get back home."*

"As long as the Brothers think that we can let out their secret, we can't do anything but hide." Her body was tense, and Joseph could almost feel the determination radiating from her. *"Unless we tell their*

secret first. Then they won't have any reason to kill us."

"They might kill us for revenge. In fact, Zarco doesn't seem like he needs a reason to kill."

"Yes, but he's going to be too busy having to hide from everybody who's looking for him."

Joseph led Chloe over to the fence when they got close and snapped his fingers. With Mayali's help he got Chloe to understand that she should relieve herself there. *"We should do what you wanted,"* said Joseph. *"Find the president. Never mind Anansi. She's a liar. She lied to us from the beginning. We don't know if anything she told us is the truth."*

"No, she's right. Things like this, you can't just depend on one person, even a president. We need everybody to know."

"What do you mean everyone?"

"Joseph, can you do the radio again?"

CHAPTER 11
Resistance Radio

C hloe growled at the door, preventing Joseph from answering. There was music playing on the other side of the door. "The boss-lady find you friend for you," the guard said.

Rafeek was inside dancing to chutney music and looking like a different person in clean clothes.

"Hey, Mayali," he said, his smile over-large. He tried to hug her, but she subtly batted his hands away. Chloe growled, but Joseph put a hand on her head and she relaxed.

"You got a dog now?" Rafeek asked. "What happen with it eye? Like it crazy or what?"

Joseph looked at him blankly.

"What you doing here?" Mayali asked Rafeek.

"That crazy Hess-Whatever lady come find me. She put me to bathe and send for buy clothes and so for me. I even get shoes." He pulled his jeans up to show them that he was wearing running shoes just like theirs.

Joseph thought to himself that Anansi must own a shoe store somewhere.

Rafeek had also gotten his hair buzzed to the scalp. He continued talking. "This place really nice though. I don't know why the lady like you, but she set y'all up good here."

"She just using we."

"For what?"

"Stop talking about Spider stuff," Joseph reminded her.

"Just ... business. She's looking to make money in gold business."

Rafeek looked at Mayali through narrowed eyes. "Okay." Then he smiled. "So, we living here now or what?"

"No. Just staying for a couple days."

"Too bad. Dracula get me kick out of me yard."

"Who?"

"That police that you push down that first day? Remember, he land in the horsesh—"

"Yeah. I remember he," Mayali said.

"He went and tell Mrs. Sobers lie, that I does use drugs in she yard." Rafeek sucked his teeth.

Joseph left them to take Chloe into his bathroom. The dog's eye needed cleaning. The dog sat still as Joseph wiped away the dried blood from around the socket with a damp towel. The eye itself was not moving about, and just sat pointing in one direction while Chloe looked about with the other.

"Joseph, we have to talk," Mayali's voice came through from the other room.

"You want to talk with Rafeek around?"

"Never mind him. I have him busy."

Joseph finished with Chloe and went to Mayali's room. He was surprised to find her in shorts and a T-shirt with a towel in her hand.

"What's this?"

"Rafeek is going to teach me to swim. He went to change his clothes."

Joseph smiled knowingly. *"You really like him, eh?"*

"Don't be stupid. He's a little boy."

Joseph smiled. *"What you want to talk to me about?"*

Mayali said, *"I want to use the National Radio tower to tell people about the Spiders. We can let everyone know at one time. The President and the army and everybody will have to decide what to do."*

"You can't just get them to interview you, and once you start talking like you're crazy, they're just going to cut you off."

"No. I want do it your way," said Mayali. *"Make your own broadcast and send it over their tower."*

Joseph shook his head. *"I don't know what their equipment is like*

*or if it will work with my computer. I don't even have my computer. I'd
need to download that program all over again and I can't —"*

*"Look, stop talking about what you can't do. Just tell me how you
can do it. Stop always being about why things can't happen."*

"I'm not always about—"

Rafeek showed up in baggy trunks that looked comical on his thin
body. "We going or what?" he asked. His ribs were visible under the
skin, but there were muscles there too. Joseph acted liked he had not
noticed the three big scars on Rafeek's side.

"Figure out what we need," Mayali said as she walked away, *"then
we'll go get it."*

Joseph was annoyed as he sat on a deck chair at the pool side
with Chloe. He kept composing explanations in his head to Mayali
for why he always objected to things. He was trying to make sure she
understood how careful she needed to be. How thorough.

In the water, Rafeek was standing in the shallow end with Mayali.
His teaching mostly involved her sputtering at some point as her head
dipped below the water.

"You'll never learn that way," said Joseph.

"What makes you think you know better?"

"I know you need to learn how to hold your breath first."

Mayali ignored him, continuing with Rafeek's lessons in floating.
Joseph walked back to his room in annoyance, but in his head he was
remembering everything he knew about commercial radio stations
and thinking of ways to hijack the signal. By the time he took Chloe
outside for one last pee before bed, he knew how he would do it.

~ ~ ~ : : ~ : ~ : : ~ ~ ~

The veterinarian, a heavy woman with boots, who looked like

she just stepped off a cow farm, showed up at 7:15 the next morning. Anansi came into the suite with her. The dog let herself be inspected as long as Joseph kept a hand on her shoulder.

"This dog been fighting," said the vet in an accusing tone.

"Is not we," said Mayali. "We just find she like this."

"This eye ... You need to give she antibiotics." The vet reached into her bag and wrote a few lines on a bottle, then she gave it to Mayali. "You follow?" the vet asked.

Joseph knew Mayali could not read, but he discovered that he could get her to send him a picture of what she saw and then he read it to her. She nodded to the vet and said, "Yeah. One tablet, twice a day with meals and water."

"Good," the vet said. "You did a good job cleaning the area. As long as you keep that up, the dog should—"

"What about him?" asked Anansi, nodding at Rafeek.

"You want me examine the boy?"

"Why not? It can't be that different."

The vet seemed like she was going to defy Anansi for a second, but then she shrugged and said to Rafeek, "Lift your shirt." The vet took a quick look at Rafeek's face, teeth and arms. "The boy look healthy. Probably got some delay in puberty due to low nutrition and he underweight and shorter than he should be. Discolouration in the eye, could be—"

"This is stupid," said Mayali. She spoke to Anansi with her mind, *"The boy isn't a pet, you know."*

"Isn't he?"

"No."

"Fine," said Anansi, then she took the vet away.

Rafeek was eager to get into the pool again and Mayali agreed to join him. Joseph went to cook breakfast. He considered just making something for himself and the dog and ignoring the other two. But they had ignored him, not even asking him to make them breakfast and so he set out to make them the best breakfast he could. Having just eggs and bread made that difficult, however. When he took the food out to the pool, Rafeek and Mayali did not seem surprised. They ran out of the water and gulped down food with 'Mmmh' and 'Aaah' sounds.

Rafeek stopped chewing long enough to say "You bring any juice?" When he remembered that Joseph could not hear, he said to Mayali, "Dumb Boy forget the juice."

"Don't call him 'Dumb Boy,'" said Mayali.

Rafeek rolled his eyes. "Alright, Joseph forget the juice."

Mayali gave him a frustrated look and then went to the kitchen and came back with a box of orange juice and three cups. Joseph took his cup and handed her a list he had written on a sheet of paper.

"What this?"

Joseph smiled.

Mayali said, *"You forget I can't read good?"*

Joseph had not forgotten. *"That's what we need to make the radio broadcast. I need to see the antenna myself to double check, but I can make it work."*

The phone in Joseph's jeans vibrated. The incoming number was the other phone that Anansi had given them, the one left at the dogfight.

"Is that Anansi?" Mayali asked.

"No."

Mayali grabbed the phone from Joseph. "Yes?" She listened for a while, she said, "No, I don't want none of that, Zarco. I want me father and if I can't get he then I want all of you dead." She cut the call off.

Rafeek looked up in alarm. "Who you want kill now? Zarco you messing with?"

"You know he?"

"I know he does kill people left, right and center. You mustn't mess with that man."

"And suppose I want you help me do it?" Mayali asked. "Fo' help me do something against Zarco?"

Joseph saw Rafeek's brow bend in fear and then flatten out. "Alright," Rafeek said. Then he smiled.

"We got to get them thing on this paper here." Mayali showed Joseph's list to him. "We might got to thief some of it like a computer. Maybe we c—"

"We can't steal," said Joseph.

"Didn't you hear what Anansi said? We can't play nice if we want to win this thing."

Rafeek said, "You need fo' have the computer or just need fo' use one? Because we can just go to a internet cafe."

Joseph felt stupid for not thinking of that.

It turned out that the rest of what they wanted could be gotten with the pocket money Anansi had given them. The internet cafe down the road had microphones that they could use. Downloading the voice software and installing it was simple. Being able to make a recording on a thumb drive took them less than a day and most of that time was working out just what information they wanted to let people know and then what questions would be used to give Mayali a chance to give that information while everything sounded like a real interview.

While they did this recording, Rafeek got them various wires, connecting cables and clips. The three of them took a side trip to look at the radio tower from up close. They walked into the National Radio Station complex and went around asking for 'Dr. Joseph Mayali' and everyone treated them politely because they looked clean and smiled and sent them to look somewhere else. They were able to inspect all the buildings that way and then left before looking too suspicious. They left a ladder in the bushes a block away after buying it at a hardware store nearby.

When they came home, the newspapers said that Father Garcia had disappeared from his hospital room and no one knew why.

Joseph had a good idea what had happened.

Anansi came to visit them that night. Mayali left Rafeek in the pool so she could talk in private with Anansi and Joseph.

"So what you going do now you have no father to look fo' and it make no sense exposing Spider?" Anansi asked Mayali.

"What you think we should do?" Mayali asked.

"The best thing for you is fo' make a life here. I can teach you the runnings, set you up with a good life. I need people I can trust fo' help me." Anansi looked at Joseph and said, "Same for you. I ain't think is safe for you go back home yet."

"We can stay here til we decide?" Mayali asked. "With Rafeek?"

"Yes, but not too long. I just doing y'all a favour."

On her way out, Anansi saw the cables near the back corner and said, "That's the stuff y'all been buying? The guard tell me about it, but I didn't realize was so much. What you planning?"

"Just something fo' make Zarco sorry about what he do to Daisy."

"Be careful. That ain't no—"

"Anansi," said Joseph, trying to distract the Spider woman. *"I need to ask you something."*

"Oh? What you need fo' know?"

"You've been alive a long time, right?"

"Yeah." Anansi looked proud. "It take a lot of brain to don't get kill for so long."

"You mentioned Jesus before. Was Jesus real? I mean, was he a real person?"

"I don't know," she said. "I never meet he. I never meet Athena neither. Or Ram or Ishtar. All we got is story what people pass down."

By this time, they had moved through the front door and Mayali had slipped out the back towards the pool. Joseph noted that she walked normally now, her ankle healed. He thanked Anansi and closed the door, then joined the others in the pool.

They left after dinner, taking a taxi into Georgetown with the last of their money. Rafeek made them put extra food into their bags. He took the front seat while Chloe got in the back with Joseph and Mayali. Rain started coming down and the driver turned on the wipers.

"I forget to buy a new knife," Mayali said.

"We won't need one."

"Always good to have a knife."

The taxi driver agreed, and he and Rafeek got into a conversation that wandered everywhere. Joseph smiled at the fact that the taxi driver never asked why Mayali needed a knife. Georgetown was a strange city and a taxi driver probably saw the strangest parts of it.

The building housing the radio center was not hard to get into. The security was not expecting an infiltration after all. The rain had stopped, in the manner of the intermittent showers that sometimes teased the city. The teens and their dog walked across the rough ground at the rear of the compound and right through a back gate that had been left open, saving them the trouble of jumping it.

"This gon' be easy," Rafeek said, shaking his head at the lax security.

"You can say that," said Mayali. "You don't have to climb nothing."

"I can climb. I can climb better than all two of you. Should be Joseph fetching this damn ladder. Is he's the strong one."

"No. Joseph can climb the best."

Joseph was surveying the building, checking that no guards were around near the corner they planned to approach. Behind him, Rafeek was still complaining.

"You know what I don't understand?" Rafeek said to Mayali. "He can't talk, but he can write and you can talk, but you can't read. So how the two of you can plan something like this? Is like you don't even need to know—"

"Shut you mouth," Mayali told him. "Run with that ladder and help Joseph get up on the roof."

The ladder was only long enough to get them to an air

conditioning unit sticking out of the wall. Joseph knew that if it could not take his weight, the whole project was over. He stepped lightly onto it and the unit bent under the force. He tried stepping as close to the inside as he could, but the same thing happened. Behind him, he heard Mayali faintly in his head asking why he wasn't going faster.

"I have to be careful," he told her. *"Relax."*

He tried a third time, even gentler than before to get a foot onto the air conditioner but it had been weakened and it separated from the wall and tumbled to the ground, landing with what Joseph was sure was a horrid crunch.

Why'd you do that?" Mayali shouted in his head. *"The guards are going to come investigate."*

"You're the one that wanted me to hurry up."

"Climb down and get away now, before they see you."

There was an iron pipe running along the side of the wall and then angled away to the rim of the roof. It was close enough that Joseph could touch it and fat enough that he felt he could get a grip. He kicked his shoes off and jumped towards the pipe, the ladder falling the other way. Between the pipe and the wooden wall was enough space for him to get a full grip and his toes were able to keep him from sliding down the slippery surface. He tried to pull himself up and that was when the pipe also gave way and he fell to the grass below, landing on his back.

Mayali and Rafeek ran passed him, carrying the ladder. *"Come on,"* said Mayali. *"The guards are coming from the other way."* Chloe stopped at his head just a moment and seemed to grin at him, then she trotted off behind the other two, as if they were playing a game. As he chased after them, Joseph thought that maybe it was over, after all that preparation, they were about to get caught and they hadn't even started. Then Mayali spotted a stair under an overhang in the roof of the building.

"This way," she said. The three of them scampered up the stairs. At

the top, they used the ladder to get Joseph onto that roof instead. Once he was up, the other two ran off, ditching the ladder behind a bench. When they were gone, Joseph circled back along the roof to where he had first tried to climb up. They had chosen that spot because it was close to where the power supply entered the building. Joseph put gloves on and removed a pair of shears. He knew that what he was about to do was possible, but to make himself hold a live wire carrying 440 volts? He hesitated. Suppose the gloves were not thick enough? And he was in his bare feet. He knew that theoretically that shouldn't matter, but who wants to test a theory when failure could get you killed?

He could see the guards below, clearly searching for the reason behind the disturbance.

He had to do this. Whatever happened he couldn't wait. Joseph, gritted his teeth and cut through the insulation. A few sparks flew and he nearly dropped the shears, but he finished the job without feeling any jolts and let out a sigh. He clipped his own line onto the exposed cable, then he ran along the snaking cable to the other side of the building where the radio antenna rose into the sky. Being on top of the building gave him easy access to the side of the tower. Now all he had to do was climb a hundred feet into the air up a wet antenna, while holding a live electrical cord.

After ten minutes of slow climbing, the weight of the cable he was carrying seemed to have doubled, but he had to be extra careful to make sure he didn't strike the end into anything. He kept it covered with insulation, but he did not want to take any chances. He lost track of time as he laboriously climbed the tower. Had he passed the spot? He looked down to check for the yellow tag on the numerous cables running up the inside of the antenna tower. He did not see one. But it was dark up here, despite the lights of the city all around him.

His muscles hurt. The height of this thing was intimidating even to him. Every time he felt his foot slip a little, he had to pause and recover his breath, and his nerve. He tried to chase his doubt away. Father Garcia was depending on him to get this done.

Joseph climbed higher, thankful that his sense of balance at least seemed to hold steady.

Soon the yellow marker was right there in his face. He made sure his feet were secure before freeing his hands and grabbing his tool—a roll of duct tape. He opened the tagged connection junction before him and disconnected the wire below. He cut the power to the antenna. Now he had to rig it the way he wanted, before anyone noticed. He brought his own wire into the junction and used the connectors and tape to secure it. He listened to the pocket radio on his cell phone which told him that the power was back on.

The climb back down was even worse than going up. He had to fight the wind to stay away from his power cable, not wanting to jar it and cause a disconnection. His neck was starting to hurt from angling it so he could look down as he descended, taking time to place each foot safely.

When he reached the bottom, the guards were waiting with their batons drawn. One of them had disconnected the cable.

CHAPTER 12

Voice to the People

After leaving Joseph on the roof, Mayali's next job was hiding. A job complicated by the dog's impatience to do something and Rafeek's even greater impatience to do something. Mayali kept Chloe close by her collar while she watched the main door from behind the bushes.

"I think Joseph need help," Rafeek said. "Some of them guards climb the roof."

"Stay here. I need help."

But Rafeek left her alone and ran off into the darkness.

Mayali watched the drama unfold on the roof. All the guards and many people in the buildings had come outside to see what was happening, all of them looking up and pointing. This was not the clandestine approach she had hoped for.

When she knew Joseph was close to the ground, she tugged on Chloe's collar. The dog seemed to respond to Mayali's mental commands.

She knew not to go for the studio when she ran in through the front door of the main building. Instead, she threw open the door to the control room. The two operators jumped out of their seats when Chloe barked and growled at them. Mayali and Chloe circled around the room, giving the frightened operators a chance to exit. She locked the door and then pushed a heavy cabinet down, blocking the doorway. Chloe stood guard. Through the glass window to the other room, Mayali watched the presenter in the studio stumble out in fear as he saw the dog.

"*Joseph, I'm ready,*" said Mayali, hoping he was close enough to hear her.

He did not respond.

"Joseph?"

"They caught me, Mayali. And they disconnected the power."

"Well, I still have power here." she said, looking around at the equipment. *"We'll stick to the plan and hope that we get most of the message out by the time they cut the power to the control room."*

With Joseph's help to read, Mayali found the master control panel and the jack for audio-in. She inserted the cable from her phone. The procedure of cutting into the normal broadcast was simply flipping a switch. The recording on her phone began to play and she could hear it through her headphones as her broadcast spread to the entire country.

First, one of Joseph's mechanical American voices started up. "Welcome, ladies and gentlemen. This is Porkknocker Paul on Radio Mabaruma and we're taking over GT. That's right, Georgetown people, tonight is the biggest night of your lives. So call you best friend. Call your mother. Call your neighbor and your dog. Tell them that the biggest news in the history of the world is about to hit and they need to tune in to 93.3 to hear it all."

Dramatic music played, like the kind that was used for the news. The welcome message played twice more, and then Pork-knocker Paul started the interview. "Our guest tonight is a young lady who came to visit from a place far, far away. How far away you ask? From a whole other world ..."

The security guards were banging on the door, but the locks held, bolstered by the fallen cabinet. Mayali went over to the glass panel in the door which looked out on the corridor. She left the interview playing – it explained how she had gotten to Earth and about the threat of the Spider gods. It would go on for about fifteen more minutes. In it she did not mention Anansi, but she mentioned that the Brothers were inside human society, working to control it and that the Spider gods intended to come to Earth and rule.

She saw the straining face of one guard as he seemed to kick at the door, but only made a loud bang. A chair swung past the pane and clanged on the door handle, but that failed too. He and several others tried to throw all their weight against it at once. That made the door quiver, but it held. One guard caught sight of her. She stuck her tongue out at him.

Mayali could hear them cursing and shouting at her. Then a woman with a screechy voice, Mayali assumed she was the supervisor, told them to cut the power to the control room. The recording continued playing even after the room went dark. The antenna was still broadcasting its signal.

It took only a minute for the supervisor to yell for the guards to cut power to the entire building. The interview kept going out even then. The supervisor cried out in frustration

"Joseph, I thought you said they disconnected the outside power from the antenna."

"They did," Joseph said.

"Then how come the signal still going out?"

"It must be Rafeek. I saw him hiding up there when they brought me down."

Because Rafeek had connected the antenna directly to the electricity from the power company, the interview kept playing. It was up to the part where Mayali mentioned the Brothers' power to trick people. It was strange for Mayali to hear her own voice like that. She sounded like someone else, more scratchy than the way she sounded to herself when she spoke.

"The guards are trying to get on the roof, but they can't climb up," Joseph said. *"Rafeek is up there with a pipe and he's hitting their fingers when they try to reach up."*

Mayali laughed as she pictured him. At that moment she realized that she not only liked the boy, but that she had only gotten as far as she had because of him.

The door crashed in, broken from the continuous attacks. The guards spilled through into the room. Chloe growled and stiffened, but Mayali held her collar. There was no point in fighting. The interview had played almost to the end. People knew about Arachne and her plans and could do something about it. She had kept her promise to Jalana. She enjoyed a deep breath. A few deep breaths, in fact.

"Where the thing you playing?" asked one guard roughly.

Mayali didn't answer. She let him hunt around, buying more time for the message to run. The guard spotted the phone plugged into the panel and reached for it.

"No, don't," said the screechy voice of the supervisor. She was a thin woman with heavy makeup and a black business suit that hung on her frame. The woman ran through the door and took the phone from the guard, setting it down.

"What you do that for?" the guard asked in a hurt voice.

"People like it."

"What?"

The supervisor turned to Mayali and said, "Young lady, I don't approve of your tactics, but that is some fine storytelling. People have been calling in for the last five minutes asking what the name of the show is and if we're going to have more episodes."

"But is not a ..."

No one believed her? Mayali gritted her teeth. She had done everything to make people take this seriously and it was just a joke to them. She wished she could reach through the radio and slap them awake.

The excited supervisor kept talking, as if Mayali had not spoken. "I even got calls from people looking to sponsor the show. This thing could be a big hit. You have excellent imagination to create something like this. I think we'll want to hire you as soon—"

"Hire me?" shouted Mayali. "Lady, this ain't no story. Everything I say is truth. Them Spider them coming to kill all y'all."

The supervisor considered Mayali for the first time and after a pause, she looked at the one-eyed dog drooling at Mayali's knee. She took three steps back to hide behind her guards.

"Mayali, it's the army," Joseph said excitedly. *"The army is here. They landed in a helicopter. It's full of soldiers."*

Mayali smiled triumphantly at the woman. The army would not come if they thought it was a joke. And if she at least got the army to believe, there was hope to get real help.

"Oh no," Joseph said. *"It's Lieutenant Dasrath."*

Mayali needed to hear no more. She pushed the guard nearest to her making him topple into another, and ripped her phone from the cord. With Chloe scaring people out of the way, she ran down the corridor. *"Time to go. We sent the message. We can't let Dasrath catch us."*

"I can't move. They handcuffed me. Hands and feet."

"Tell me where you are," Mayali said. *"I'll come get you."*

"No. You have the recording with you?"

"Yes." Mayali was out the front door. The soldiers were running around the corner of the building, probably to where Joseph was.

"Keep it and run. You have to find somebody who will believe you."

The helicopter was parked on the grass, rotor spinning loudly, in the space between the two main buildings. Mayali paused, assessing her next move. As she watched the helicopter she recognized Tara seated beside the pilot, her expression a combination of fright and excitement. Mayali decided to circle out of her sight, but the other girl saw her and started calling to her. Even if her voice was drowned by the engine's noise, with the girl waving and looking in her direction, Mayali knew someone was sure to suspect something.

Mayali decided to run. Tara jumped out of the helicopter and chased after her, catching up to Mayali as they hit the street. The helicopter pilot was shouting at Tara to come back, but he did not seem ready to leave his aircraft and chase her.

"Where we going?" Tara seemed able to run and talk without

panting.

Mayali was out of breath and her ankle hurt. Even Chloe was taking big breaths.

"I got to get away from Dasrath. He gon' lock me up." Homestretch Avenue had only a few headlights to the west so Mayali ran east, towards the street lamps at the junction with Sheriff Street which seemed even brighter as the lights reflected off the wet road.

"I know. He had me lock up the last week. Nobody else here? Joseph?"

Rafeek came flying over the fence and landed with a splash in the ditch. He sputtered and grinned and clambered out, dripping from his new haircut right down to his new shoes. "Hurry up people, we got—"

Police sirens came around the bend and a car with flashing lights squealed through the intersection. There was nowhere to run except across the canal into the dangerous dark of the Botanical Gardens. Mayali hesitated before she decided she would leave Rafeek and Tara behind. But the delay cost her the chance. The car skidded to a stop, blocking her way, and three officers got out, two women and a man.

"That is he," the man shouted. "I know a criminal like he had to be part of this." It was the big-toothed policeman that Rafeek had called Dracula. Rafeek tried to run, but the other two police officers grabbed him. Dracula took Rafeek by the elbow and wrist and pressed him face down into the road with a knee in his back.

The boy grunted, holding back his pain.

Mayali grabbed the policeman's arm and tried to yank him off. She shouted, "Stop it, Dracula! Leave him—"

He pushed her weight off and glared at her. "What you call me?"

She checked her memory to see if she had gotten the name wrong. "Officer Dracula. That's not you?"

The other police officers were laughing.

"He name not Dracula," said Rafeek. "Don't make he vex."

"You say he was Dracula."

"That's not he real name. He just look like that freaky monster in the movie is all."

"What movie?" Mayali asked.

Officer Dracula drew his baton from his belt, rising towards Mayali with hate in his eyes. But then his jaw dropped in alarm and the weapon slipped from his hand. Four men walked into the light. It was Zarco and his gang. They must have heard the radio broadcast too. With them were two dogs on leashes. A black Navigator with tinted windows was parked behind them.

Dracula stood and saluted. "Good night, Commander," he said to Zarco. The other two officers did the same.

Zarco returned the salute. In Mayali's eyes, he was wearing the same clothes as at the dogfight and his men were in Brothers' robes. "Is everything in order?" asked Zarco. "Are you following procedures?"

"Uh, yes, sir," said Dracula. "This suspect was resisting arrest so we had to use some force to—"

"I want you to hand over these prisoners to me," Zarco said.

"Of course, sir," said one of the officers, her voice full of respect.

"You can't hand we over to them," said Mayali. "He's one of the Spider Brother I tell you about on the radio. You can't see?" She pointed at Zarco. "Look. Look good."

Smiling, Zarco said, "Mayali, you got to stop making up story like this."

There was the screech of brakes and a taxi hurtled towards them. Zarco and his men jumped to the roadside as it ploughed into the police car. It was the same taxi that had brought them and the driver was yelling for them to get in. Could Mayali trust him? Zarco was back on his feet, yelling for his men to grab her. Mayali jumped into the car with Tara and the dog. She looked to call for Rafeek, but could not see him.

"What you doing here?" she asked the driver as he accelerated down the road.

"The boss lady say wait for you."

"You work for Anan— You work for Miss Hiladora?"

"Yes," said the driver. "Where Joseph?"

Mayali started to lie, but Tara surprised her. "He get lock up," the other girl said in a quiet voice.

CHAPTER 13
Operation Kaieteur

Joseph stood at the edge of the steep canyon carved into the Potaro river by Kaieteur, the massive waterfall pouring like a thousand foot veil over a vertical cliff. Mist floated up out of the chasm, glowing and wet. Six days had passed since his capture at the radio station. It was just after dinner now and the last of the tourist planes had left, so Joseph was allowed outside. He was still being detained after all. In this spot, a hundred and thirty miles from Georgetown, surrounded by the jungle and its denizens, he faced a paradoxical life of being free to roam all of his prison.

He wished Mayali could see the waterfall, glittering under the moonlight. Kaieteur was broad as well as tall. The soldiers complained about its unceasing, rushing noise. Mayali would be amazed by it. Thinking about Mayali made him remember that Tara was still missing. Joseph sighed.

Dasrath tapped him on the shoulder and indicated it was time to head back. They walked over the loose stones, Joseph's new army boots crunching as it pressed on them. The card game was starting. Joseph could not ever remember playing so much. The game of the table was Rap, played for five and ten-dollar coins. Joseph had bought into the game with a loan from Sergeant Collins, but now had a good pocket of change he'd grown out of it.

At least fourteen soldiers under Lieutenant Dasrath's command had set up a camp in one of the old guesthouses near the Kaieteur site. In the week since Joseph had been taken prisoner, however, there were never more than five soldiers around at any time, different soldiers were leaving and returning on the helicopter at random hours of the night. The helicopter never stayed long, only refueling and reloading at Kaieteur. Where and when the pilot slept, Joseph did not know. The soldiers stayed out of sight during the day too, almost as if they too were prisoners. The caretaker of the guesthouse brought them meals. He and Dasrath seemed to be old friends.

Sergeant Collins, a short young woman with her hair in a perpetual bun, took charge whenever Dasrath was away. She had a friendly, smiling approach to being Joseph's jailer and had invited him to the card table which the soldiers used to keep themselves busy in the boring hours they spent in the house before going off to do whatever it was they did for Dasrath when they left. The first night of cards moved Joseph from tolerated burden to celebrated guest as he kept the money flowing his way, impressing the soldiers. He still had to spend the day in a guest bedroom, but it was a cool room with two large wooden windows that swung open. He could escape out of them at any time, but then again, the door was unlocked too. The bed was comfortable and he even had a shelf of old novels that previous visitors had left behind.

Tonight's after-dinner gathering was the largest so far, with ten soldiers, and they had not broken open the cards as yet. Instead they talked in pairs or threes with expectant glances at Lieutenant Dasrath. The lieutenant inspected the soldiers' equipment and asked a few questions before taking Joseph into the living room. A map hung on the wall along with lists of numbers and items that Joseph had read, but did not quite comprehend. Army stuff. Two heavy laptop computers sat on a round dinner table in the middle. They showed more maps and army stuff. Joseph had tried to get a closer look at the machines, but Sergeant Collins smiled and moved him away every time.

Dasrath brought over two cups of coffee from the kitchen and indicated that Joseph should sit. The soldier wrote a note on a pad and handed it over. The message was, "Tomorrow is it. I need to ask you some serious questions tonight."

Joseph drank a few sips before he wrote back, "You already know everything. It was on the radio." Joseph had been saying this to Dasrath all week, but the man kept asking him to repeat things. Occasionally, Dasrath would show him pictures of camps or waterfalls which had been taken at a low angle from far away and ask him if he knew anything about them. Dasrath got frustrated at his negative replies, but seemed to be working hard to keep his temper. Joseph knew that the soldiers were in the Kaieteur area looking for the Brothers in some way, but no one told him anything else.

"You sure you can identify Brothers?" Dasrath wrote. "You must be sure!!!"

Joseph noted the number of exclamation points at the end of the message.

"Yes. I can see their real self. Except for Zarco. Don't know what he looks like."

Dasrath pulled up photos of a waterfall which seemed large, judging by the size of the trees growing all around it. A road was under construction and a camp of about a dozen low buildings lined the end of the road. Yellow dump trucks and excavators were parked everywhere.

"This is where they are," Dasrath wrote. "Amaila Falls."

"How you know?"

Dasrath paused as if considering multiple versions of truth and then turned a computer to face Joseph. He pulled up a satellite map of the Mabaruma area and photographs of a camp on the river. He wrote, "This is Brothers' Mabaruma camp. Found it after talk with Mayali. Look at tree colours."

Joseph shook his head because he could see nothing significant.

Dasrath took the mouse and a new version of the map photo used dots to highlight all the dozens of trees whose leaves had a brownish tint. The dots formed eight lines fanning out from a central point, each one about twenty trees in length. At the junction of the lines was the pool where the camp was found. It was also the pool Mayali had climbed out of six months earlier.

"Passage to other world," wrote Dasrath. "Draining water out of forest by magic." Dasrath showed Joseph nine other places on different maps with the same eight-lined pattern of brown trees. All of the lines met in rivers or ponds. Those sites were unused, however. Finally, Dasrath showed the satellite view of the Amaila waterfall with the camp and construction equipment. The eight lines were massive, easily a hundred trees long and five trees wide, and centered on the waterfall.

"70 workers," wrote Dasrath. "Supposed to be govt hydro project for electricity. But not really govt."

"Brothers?" Joseph pointed to the picture and shrugged. He missed being able to speak with the detail and fluency of the Spider's Touch. The slowness of improvised signs and writing made his muscles twitch.

Dasrath wrote, "You will check prisoners for Brothers. Stay on helicopter until needed."

Joseph smiled at the idea that Lieutenant Dasrath was making him a part of his mission. The first day after Joseph had been captured at the radio station, he had been kept in a concrete cell at Army Headquarters in Georgetown. Dasrath had glowered at him the entire time while asking him written questions. Joseph requested his parents, but Dasrath refused. Joseph told him that was illegal, but Dasrath simply kept asking questions about the Brothers and what he and Mayali had done. Joseph told the truth, except that he did not mention Anansi. Mayali had escaped the radio station and he did not want Dasrath finding her by tracing the Spider woman. Instead, Joseph had lied and said Rafeek had told them about Zarco. He said they had slept at Rafeek's house and the boy had stolen money and new clothes for them.

Between the information from Mayali's broadcast and the helicopter flights, however, Dasrath had learned enough to ease his frustrations and he relaxed. The move to Kaieteur had helped also. He and Joseph had gotten into the habit of taking evening walks under the rationale that the prisoner needed exercise.

Now, Dasrath was depending on him to help fight the Brothers. It had been a strange week.

Joseph wanted to let Dasrath know about Anansi, but was afraid to admit he had lied. It would not matter in any case. Anansi was not working with the Brothers. Joseph saw Lieutenant Dasrath looking contemplatively at his coffee. He patted the man on his back and wrote, "You a good man. Working hard to make things safe."

Dasrath shook his head. "No," he wrote. "Done a lot bad." Dasrath bit his lip and added. "There's a reason my wife left me and took son."

Joseph regretted this conversation. He had picked up scraps of Dasrath's past from the soldiers during the card games, references to alcohol, violence and a demotion – as well as brilliance, skill and leadership. Joseph had come to like Dasrath enough to tolerate being conscripted into Dasrath's personal army. Learning the darker truths about the man might cause doubt.

Dasrath must have sensed the awkward air and wrote, "Never mind me. Go play cards. Bed early."

The game lacked spirit that night, though, with everyone dwelling on the next day's raid. Joseph abandoned it and stood in the centre of his room, wondering what the rest of the world would think if they knew what he was doing, preparing to fly into a camp of invaders from another world. Then he realized with disgust that no one would believe him. According to Dasrath, the country had laughed at Joseph's Spider revelations on the radio. There had been a few people talking about how it had to be real, but most of them had ended up laughing at themselves and admitting they had been fooled by a good joke. A few still believed, some even producing evidence and testimony of encounters with Brothers, but everyone treated them like crazy people.

At least the Army believed, Joseph noted. And once Dasrath's attack on the hydro dam captured a few Brothers, the world would have to take it all very seriously and act. Then Joseph could go home again. And so could Father Garcia once the Brothers revealed where he was.

~ ~ ~ : : ~ : ~ : : ~ ~ ~

They awoke before dawn, everyone calmly packing the helicopter while Joseph ate a cheese sandwich and drank coffee. At one point, Joseph noticed that everyone was too busy to notice him and he sat sideways to a laptop and calmly checked the news on the camp's satellite link internet. A screen Joseph found caused him to pause. It was Dasrath's army e-mail account. Joseph read through the most recent message.

FROM: COL. SIMEON H. FRANKLYN, C.O. 3RD INF BATTALION
TO: LIEUT. J. K. DASRATH, MABARUMA DETACHMENT
SUBJECT: YOU ARE IN VIOLATION OF ORDERS

Kishan,

Given what you say, I can't imagine this will end well if you pursue it. Everything you have done up to now can be construed as an attack of zeal, even stealing the army's helicopter. We can write it off as you acting on bad information, but if you take action against this site you found, you will make a public spectacle of yourself and I imagine the consequences will not end with the demise of your career. You will be seeing the inside of a jail cell for many years.

As your friend and superior, I think this would be –

Joseph got to read no further because Sergeant Collins caught sight of him and slammed the computer closed. With her pleasant smile still in place, she shook her head, pointed to her watch and made a motion for Joseph to follow her.

Outside the guesthouse, the helicopter's rotors were spinning and everyone was strapping in. Counting Dasrath and Joseph, there were nine passengers. Joseph's second ride in the helicopter was much more enjoyable than the first. This time he was not disoriented from lack of sleep and the dark of a prison cell. And he was no longer afraid of the people around him.

Dawn's light struck the helicopter in mid-flight, hurting Joseph's eyes. Below them, pockets of shadow resisted the sun's challenge among the trees growing on the steep mountainsides. The aircraft followed the mottled valley of the Potaro River and within minutes it was at the Amaila encampment. The steep descent made Joseph want to vomit and he eventually did when the helicopter swung up wildly before touching down. The soldiers scrambled out in an instant and then the pilot flung the helicopter into the sky again, rising to about a hundred feet off the ground and circling.

From there, Joseph saw the soldiers spread out and sweep into the camp. They entered the buildings in groups of three or four and herded workers out, many in their underwear. No one was resisting.

A few flashes of light showed gunfire to the west, near the waterfall itself. Someone was shooting at the soldiers. The pilot jerked the helicopter away and Joseph strained to see more as it turned. Within a few minutes the helicopter had come back around and

Joseph could see four soldiers charging at the guard positions, Dasrath in the lead. Four other soldiers emerged from the trees to the north, pinning the guards in a crossfire. With no hope of winning, the guards dropped their weapons, putting their hands over their heads. There were about ten of them in all.

Joseph watched from the air as Dasrath's team secured the work camp, herding the compliant workers into a central square while the armed guards were made to kneel in a line, their legs shackled and chained. The helicopter landed in a swirl of dust on the stony ground, a pungent smell much like burnt matches coming with it. Dasrath came straight to Joseph when he stepped off the helicopter and grabbed the boy's elbow, dragging him to the captured guards. Their guns lay in a pile to the side, the magazines removed, with a corporal standing over them. With glee on his face, Dasrath pointed to the men.

Joseph looked them over. They were not local. They were too light skinned and sunburnt. He walked around them, taking sudden steps and sudden stops to try and provoke the flicker in his vision that would unmask the Brothers in the group, letting him see them in their robes. The men at first seemed apprehensive of Joseph's inspection, recoiling when he moved near. Eventually, though, they started to smile and then chuckle, speaking to each other in short sentences.

Dasrath slapped one of them across the face, startling Joseph, who jumped sideways. The lieutenant shouted at the group of men, spit flying as he pointed at the camp around them. When he was done, Dasrath took a few deep breaths, backed away and turned to Joseph. 'Well,' he gestured with his hands.

Joseph shook his head.

Dasrath wrote a note for him on a scribble pad he ripped from a pouch on his army belt. "You sure they not Brothers?"

"Sure," Joseph told him. "No head buzz. No robes."

Dasrath threw the notepad to the ground and yelled something through gritted teeth. The man walked away, kicking at the loose stones on the ground. The captured men looked at each other blinking and sweating. Joseph shared their disquiet. Dasrath and his soldiers had bet their careers that this was a Brothers camp and now they had lost.

CHAPTER 14

Escape

ayali had been waiting seven days for Anansi to get rid of her. The Spider woman had almost kicked her out the night after the radio broadcast, telling her it had been irresponsible to go public.

"You can't just do everything in one big swoop," Anansi said, as they stood in her living room.

Yet as Mayali stared at the ocean glittering under the moonlight outside the massive window, her heart was still thumping from the escape. She had no time for talk of taking things slow. She wanted to go back to the radio station and find Rafeek. She wanted to set Joseph free. Most of all, she wanted to put her hands on Zarco's fat neck and … there she was unsure. She had never gotten to the point of murder and the mechanics of it seemed hazy to her. But whatever it was she intended, it meant catching Zarco.

But Anansi wanted her to be timid. "You got fo' take step one, then step two, then step three, and so on," Anansi told her. "If you want win this thing, you—"

"That's why you been here two thousand year and never do nothing."

"I done save this world a dozen time already!"

"Save yourself you mean."

Anansi smiled. "Ain't no difference, really." She looked at her watch and let out a deep breath. "You upsetting my work, Mayali. The Brothers gon' panic now over this kind of sudden move. They gon' know they get lucky nobody believe you. But they know you working for Jalana, which mean they want kill you now, not just catch you and send—"

"I don't work for nobody. I just looking for me father and a way fo' live in peace."

"What you saying? You gon' stop trying fo' warn people about Spider?"

Mayali took a breath and looked down. "Yes."

"Yes?" Anansi raised one of her delicately trimmed eyebrows.

Mayali looked up, resentful of Anansi's ability to figure her out. "No. I promise Jalana I would get help."

"Well, you see? The best thing fo' you do is run. I think Suriname would be a good start. Or French Guiana. Gon' be easy to find a way fo' get to Europe going through one of them."

"They don't have Brother in Europe?"

"A thousand. More even. But they not expecting you."

Mayali returned to her room to find Chloe and Tara had fallen asleep on the floor of her bedroom. Being tired herself, she did not wake them, and got into the bed. She awoke with Chloe and Tara snuggled against her back.

She gasped in disgust at the dog's breath and left to find breakfast. Her cooking had not improved, so it was cereal and toast. She had learned to operate the pop-up toaster at least. Tara joined her in the kitchen soon after and fried herself three eggs. The dog sat patiently and it was not until Tara had Chloe lick the scraps off her plate that Mayali realized the dog needed to be fed. It was cereal and toast for Chloe as well.

The television showed a morning program where the hosts were laughing about the Spider incident the night before. Most people had not been listening to the radio, but the station was replaying parts of the broadcast to let people know what the joke was. The television people were praising the originality of the story. One said the boldness of the 'reality format' was the kind of innovation that might make radio popular again.

"Spider," said Tara with annoyance, as she lumped down on the couch. "The whole time with Dasrath was just Spider this and Spider that. Fed up with damn Spider."

"It real though," Mayali told her. "The whole story true."

"I know is true." Tara picked up the remote and switched channels. "I still fed up with it backside."

Mayali smiled at the half-curse and said, "You don't go to church regular? I don't think I ever see you there."

Tara grunted. "I got work every Saturday night. Don't done 'til three, four in the morning. Church time is sleep time for me. Besides, the Father does run when he see me. Too much headache."

"You work at Shelly Bar?"

"Yeah. Waitressing."

"Hard work?"

"Sometimes. Depend how hard you want make it for yourself." Tara lowered her voice, like she was telling a secret. "Some of them girls does take the men to the back room and make them happy for extra money. Not me though. But some of them men when they drunk does think that they can put they hand pon me whenever and wherever and I don't want make them vex, so I does just slide out and move way."

"But you should stop them if you don't like it," Mayali said puzzled.

"Nah, I need them fo' spend money. Shelly is me sister. I get a share out of everything she make."

"Oh," said Mayali. "So your sister make the girls go with the men?"

"Nah. She don't have to. They keep the extra money for themself. Buy new phone and sequin belt and what not."

"But Shelly allow them fo' use the place?"

"Well, if the man happy, they does spend money pon liquor."

"Sound stupid," Mayali said, shrugging. "I can't work a job like that."

"A lot of people can't handle it. You got fo' be nice without being stupid."

A shark movie was on one of the channels. "So how old is you?" Mayali asked.

"Eighteen." Then as if she knew the next question from experience, she added, "I left school at fourteen. Went and work with Shelly right after."

On screen, a woman in diving gear was swimming away from a monstrous shark that moved through the water like a bullet. The motions of both fish and human captivated Mayali. Mostly, the idea of being under such deep water fascinated her. How would that feel? Being in the pool had given her a sense of freedom. Water without bottom like that would seem like a place of endless possibilities.

Thinking of swimming reminded her of Rafeek. She was sure the boy had escaped. Maybe she should ask Anansi to check for him again? No. Asking Anansi for things was not wise.

As if answering the call of her name, Anansi came to visit.

"Joseph at the Army Headquarter," she said. "So far he only repeating what been on the broadcast. Nothing about me."

"So, they gon' let he go?" Tara asked.

"No. They still investigating. I trying to pressure me contacts though, see if they can't let him out early."

"You got contacts in the army?" Mayali asked.

Anansi smiled. "I got contacts everywhere, including the passport office in every country. I getting you a Dutch passport. Gon' take a week to arrive." Anansi handed a camera to Tara. "Here, take she picture."

Tara complied, handing the camera back to Anansi as soon as she was finished. "You giving the dog the medicine for she eye?" Anansi asked.

Mayali groaned. She looked over at the dog, who was lying in front of the television watching the shark eat a boat, her one good eye moving to follow the action.

Anansi shook her head in disapproval and left.

Mayali went and got the medicine. Convincing the dog to take the pills was difficult and Mayali was too scared to put her hand near the dog's mouth.

"Just grind it up in she food," Tara suggested. The dog sniffed the bowl suspiciously, but accepted the medicine that way. After the shark movie, Tara and Mayali played cards and watched more television, hardly talking. For Mayali it was like failing at the radio station, after putting so much hope into it, had flattened her will to fight. And if the stupid people in this country were making a joke out of her life, well, maybe they deserved to get invaded and conquered. The night before she was revved up for action - now going away to Suriname seemed like the best thing.

On the morning of the second day, Mayali stopped on her way to the kitchen because of a foul smell. One of the empty bedrooms had become Chloe's toilet. Joseph had always taken Chloe for walks to let her drop her loads in the backyard. It seemed that Mayali would have to take over that duty. But first she had to clean the room. Tara helped a little at first, but said she couldn't take it anymore and left. It was a disgusting task, but it was something to do.

Mayali allowed Tara to take her into Georgetown and buy DVDs. She wanted to see another shark movie, and while they were downtown, she could check Rafeek's yard. When they got there the yard seemed abandoned. The trip to select a movie kept Mayali's mind off yet another failure.

"You know, you's the only person that ain't ask how I end up with Joseph. Most people think it strange," Tara said while the two of them were sifting through titles.

"It don't seem important. You like one another. Is not complicated." Mayali eyed one DVD cover with a picture of a giant shark with tentacles growing out of its chest. "You think them movie does show real thing?" she asked Tara.

"Got to be," said Tara. "I mean, it look real."

The two of them spent their days watching movies and talking about them, Tara often picked movies she felt would appeal to Mayali.

Watching the movies, Mayali wasn't sure how to express the idea that Tara had been considerate. Before her father left, she'd had friends. But it had been over a year now of running and fighting, not staying in one place long enough to make friends, and not with anyone close to her age.

"I don't get it. Nobody didn't get eat," Mayali said to Tara over a lunch of beef stew that Tara had cooked. They had turned to the documentary after Mayali had stated her disappointment with the film.

"You want see people get eat?"

"Yes."

"But that was real life. The people would dead for real."

"Oh," said Mayali. "So the movie ain't real, but the documentary real? How they make the documentary?"

"I don't know," said Tara. "But, if you want see people get eat, you need to see a piranha movie."

"Piranha?"

"Some little fish, but like a thousand of them does attack you one time. Clean you bones by the time they done with you."

The waters in this world were teeming with life, Mayali realized.

Each time they went to the pirated DVDs stall, Mayali made sure to check for Rafeek. He was never there and Mrs. Sobers said she had not seen him.

Anansi visited with news. Joseph had been kidnapped, taken by Dasrath in a stolen helicopter and no one knew where he was. Mayali walked the dog and spent the afternoon playing cards with Tara, telling her about Zolpash and the Brothers and life among the rocksliders and escaping to Guyana. Being with Tara was mending her disappointment over the radio station failure. Not everyone in this country was an idiot after all. And just doing nothing with Tara was making her relaxed.

After watching the spectacle of blood and water that was the piranha movie, they played cards again. Mayali was finding the game more and more boring. She asked Tara, "So what you gon' do now? Go back home?"

"I don't really feel like going back. I fed up dealing with my sister and Anansi say she could give me a job up here."

"What kind?"

"Sales clerk. She own a couple fashion store, selling clothes and shoes and so on."

Mayali chucked in her cards and looked at Tara. "You think I should go? Suriname, I mean."

"People want fo' kill you here. You don't think you should go?"

"But then they gon' win."

"And if you stay, you gon' dead," Tara said. "You should save yourself now and try again later."

Mayali left the cards and sat on the carpet near Chloe, petting the dog's ear. Chloe licked her ankle. It felt disgusting to Mayali, but not disgusting enough for her to stop it.

That night Zarco phoned. Mayali picked up the third call. "What you want?"

"I want see you scream and dead. I want see you carcass dry up in the heat and turn to dust."

"Nothing better you ain't got fo' do than call me and tell me stupidness?"

"I gon' find you. I gon' find you buck man friend. I gon' find that li'l rat what helping you. I gon' find all y'all. Nobody don't get away from me."

Mayali smiled, realizing that Rafeek was still safe. "If you could do it, you would done do it already."

She hung up and set the ringer on silent.

A text message came through. "Run," it said.

On the sixth day, Anansi brought her Dutch passport. She would provide a car to take Mayali to the Corentyne ferry the next afternoon, there to cross into Suriname. The document seemed oddly powerful, especially with her photograph on it. It was the only photograph ever taken of her and it did not look at all like she imagined herself, but this was a new life, so maybe it was right that she looked different. Her name was Anna Averesch now.

But she still felt like Mayali.

By noon on Sunday Chloe's fate was still undecided.

"I think you should take the dog," Tara said. "She like you more than me."

"No. That not true." Mayali looked at Chloe who was sniffing at her packed suitcase. "Me?"

"Yesterday, I try take she for she walk and she refuse. And remember when I—"

The door opened and Rafeek walked in, looking like he'd crawled out of a gutter. His clothes were rumpled and his shirt torn. His shoes were missing and his eyes looked dry and red.

"Where you been?" Mayali demanded.

But Rafeek was too tired to quarrel and took water from the fridge. After a few swallows, he said, "I been following Zarco."

"You crazy? That man would kill you."

"I find you father, Mayali."

She said nothing. Was this one of Rafeek's jokes? He looked too tired to joke. Even his voice had a sort of desperate sincerity. "Where?" she asked. "How?"

"The water treatment plant. Zarco people run that place. The one on Vlissingen Road. He got a set of people lock up in there. I see you father. The man from the ID card."

"You sure? You talk to he?"

"I couldn't get close. But is he face for sure. Plus the building got that sign you tell me about, them eight triangle join together."

"The mark of Arrak."

"Yeah." Rafeek looked at her with more of that desperate air.

"Mayali, them thing pon the radio about the Spider and all that? That true?"

"Yes," Mayali said, forcing herself to keep eye contact.

Rafeek seemed pained. He said, "And you never tell me?"

"I didn't tell anybody. Even Joseph only find out by accident."

Rafeek looked around, saw the dog and said, "We got to go now, Mayali. They moving them people around all the time. I ain't know where they gon' carry them next. We got to go. Bring the dog and let me and you go."

"No, we can't take the dog."

"We gon' need help. Let she come."

Mayali said to Tara, "You want come too?"

"I gon' help you, yes."

Mayali looked at them and then looked over at her suitcase. "I got to go talk to Anansi. Y'all wait here."

Getting to Anansi in the middle of the day involved convincing her secretary to let her into the Hiladora factory office. Mayali's impatience grew in what seemed like the age that passed before a gaggle of businessmen left the meeting room. Anansi was sitting on one of the sofas, her attention fixed on a tablet.

"Rafeek say he see me father."

"Rafeek see wrong," Anansi said without looking up from the screen.

"He say Zarco got him at the water plant. I need to go check," she paused. "Or you could check for me."

"I had a suspicion they using that water place for something," Anansi said, looking up for the first time since Mayali entered the room.

"They holding people there."

"Well one of them resemble you father, that's all. Is five years now you ain't seen him. He could stand up right in front of you and you self wouldn't know he. How Rafeek—"

"I would know he, yes!"

"Alright. Sorry," Anansi said. She softened her tone. "I can—"

Anansi's phone rang. She looked at the number and signalled Mayali to wait. Mayali ground her teeth together. What if they moved her father while Anansi kept her waiting?

"What wrong with that man?" Anansi said angrily to the person on the other end of her phone. "He don't understand they got time and place for everything? You take you time setting up something and some idiot jump too fast and mess it up. That goddamn Dasrath. I gon' call you back. I need to rearrange a couple thing." Anansi muttered to herself as she flicked through her phone. "People don't understand what it take to build something."

Mayali almost laughed at the way Anansi's rage had her talking half to Mayali and half to herself. The Spider woman continued her grievance. "A web got a thousand piece and you got fo' put them down one piece after another. Put them down soft. It take patience. You got to balance everything. You can't just shoot it out you backside all one time. Some people can't—"

Anansi seemed to remember Mayali was still there and looked up from her phone. "I need help now," Mayali said.

"I got to go. And you got to go too. Just go get ready to leave. I gon' send a car for you. And I gon' send some people to check out the water plant." Anansi left the office, tapping at her phone as she went.

Rafeek was waiting outside the factory with the dog.

"Where Tara?" Mayali asked.

"She decide to wait in case Joseph come back."

"Alright, " Mayali said, though she was a little hurt that Tara had changed her mind. The girl had started to become a comfort to have around. They took a car, the taxi driver charging them triple to take the dog and threatening to charge them for damages if the dog messed on anything. Chloe spent the ride happily breathing against the nervous driver's neck from the back seat. Mayali smiled at that, glad that Rafeek had insisted she bring the dog along. Chloe made her feel safer.

In the front seat, Rafeek was getting impatient with the driver, letting him know well ahead of time when to turn and which streets would get them there faster.

"Hey, man!" the driver finally said. "I work taxi in this town nineteen year now. Don't tell me how fo' drive."

Rafeek stayed quiet and bit his nails to keep from talking.

The headquarters of Georgetown Water Company was an unfenced compound of about ten buildings on Church Street. It sat alongside the wide Lama Canal from which it drew the city's water supply and distributed it in all directions. No guard hassled them or even seemed to notice them as they walked in through the parking lot and around to the back.

"You sure about this?" Mayali asked.

"They take them into a store room over behind that building."

The door was padlocked on the outside. Mayali looked around. The angles of the buildings meant that no one could see them. And the ground was full of metal pipes. She grabbed one, telling Rafeek to check for anyone watching. When he gave the all clear, she brought it down on the latch, knocking it askew. Chloe whined at the sound. Another blow and the latch broke.

Inside was a dark corridor leading to a set of stairs. They went down three stories with rooms at each landing. Rafeek's hand on her back made Mayali press forward until they found the final floor. One corridor opened into the top of a dark chamber as large as the Hiladora factory. The floor was far below, at least four stories, though Mayali could not get a good view without getting closer. Right in front of her was a door. Rafeek bumped into her from behind and they moved together towards it.

Chloe growled loudly, the sound reverberating in the stairwell. This door had a latch on the outside and it opened freely into a lighted room that smelled of stale human waste. There were two other doors, one to each side, both closed. Six men and two women sat half naked on the concrete floor, looking up in fear and surprise. Immediately, Mayali recognized Father Garcia, his torso strapped with dirty bandages. The man smiled at her, but said nothing.

"Mayali?" said another man. It was Jamesy. She ran over to him, seeing him tied by cloth strips to a hoop in the ground. As she freed him, he said, "You shouldn't have come. Them people this wicked. They evil. Don't—"

"I ain't evil." Zarco, his eyes masked by his blue sunglasses, stood behind them in the doorway they had just entered. "I just making the best out of life. If more people would stand up for they self like me, evil couldn't touch them." More men appeared behind Zarco, wearing the hoods and robes of Brothers and carrying nets with heavy rings around the edges.

Chloe charged past Rafeek at the Brothers, but they dropped the nets over her. She ripped at the strands with her teeth and claws, but two other Brothers arrived and they used nooses on sticks to trap her further.

"Quiet," Mayali commanded, not wanting the dog to waste energy.

"Yes," Zarco said as the dog settled. "Quiet. It gon' be real quiet soon."

CHAPTER 15

Joseph Goes to Confession

On the ground at the camp, Joseph stayed close to Lieutenant Dasrath, communicating with notes and signals. Sergeant Collins had established that the guards were Brazilian. She spoke Portuguese and interviewed them separately. Each man said he had been recruited in Boa Vista to guard the work site against thieves and wild animals. They had been ordered to have no contact with the workers and only interacted with 'the boss', a man who was currently missing.

Upon hearing this, Dasrath sent four of his soldiers to check for hiding places.

The workers looked like typical locals, but spoke no language that anyone could figure out. No English words got a response out of them. Joseph got Dasrath to try the word 'Guatrachi' in private with a few men and they all became either scared or angry.

This was no innocent construction site.

Confirmation came when one of the soldiers reported they had found a tunnel entrance under one of the dormitories. Three soldiers stayed behind to guard the workers. Joseph walked behind Dasrath and the other soldiers, entering each room along the tunnel only after they inspected it.

The air smelled like burnt matches and garlic. Joseph recognized it as sulphur. Everything was brightly lit. The lighting fixtures and wires were installed securely and neatly. Everything was clean. The walls were cut out of rock and used few metal and concrete supports. In all, they found about thirty rooms in a complex of interconnected corridors. Most were filled with pipes and industrial equipment with a few holding computers and desks. All the corridors converged at the other side, leading into a cavern. Four giant generators were in the large chamber, vibrating as they worked. Huge pipes, twice his height in diameter, fed into them and then back out, gushing dark water into a pool sitting against a large, blank wall. It seemed that the hydropower project had been completed here, underground. The sulphurous smell was rising off the water.

They found no exit. But these four generators were far too powerful for just the rooms they had found. The soldiers must have overlooked a section in their exploration. Dasrath took the men back the way they came, probably to search for just such a missed door. He signalled Joseph to stay.

There was plenty of room to walk about in the generator room. Joseph got as close as he could to the hydro engines, surprised by how few parts actually moved. He noticed that the ground was clear of the obstructions and tools. Whoever operated this equipment was a professional. A wall of gauges showed how the engines were performing. He added up the totals in his mind and realized that the electricity in the plant could probably power half the country.

He followed the water outflow from the engine back to the pool and wondered why the water was not rising. Was it flowing back into the river at some point?

A movement almost outside his periphery vision caught his attention and he saw a strange translucent blob the size of a hippopotamus drop to the ground with a plop. The thing was mostly round and slid along the floor in squishy motions. It was darker at the center, with lines radiating outward. It seemed it was only being held together by a speckled skin, and as it went through deeper shadows, it glowed. This had to be a rockslider, Joseph thought. It must have escaped notice earlier by hiding in the pipes and catwalks of the ceiling.

The creature pressed a part of itself against the wall and the concrete cracked open on a vertical line, revealing a door. The rockslider squeezed through. After the door closed, Joseph walked over to the spot to see where the controls were. Two carved symbols marked slight rises in the rock wall. Joseph dared not touch them. He turned around intending to report to Lieutenant Dasrath, but the rockslider grabbed from behind, its liquid touch cold on his arms. Joseph had been unable to hear the door opening. He was pulled inside, then tossed to the floor.

He was in another humongous cavern, drowning in the sulphur smell. At the end near Joseph was a rectangular pool of churning water. Ramps zig-zagged up to a central platform supporting a black metal arch. A house could have fit between its legs. Electric sparks coiled randomly about the curve of the arch. Water pipes, smaller than the ones in the other room, led from the pool into the archway where they disappeared into the far wall. Barrels and crates were organized in neat stacks around the room. The hidden door he had been pulled through shut behind him.

The rockslider was the only one in the room with Joseph. It had nothing he could consider eyes, mouth or even face. It seemed to change direction without looking or turning as it navigated the ramp to the central platform. Joseph knelt, hiding behind a crate. It seemed the rockslider hadn't wanted to kill him, just keep him from warning the soldiers, but he was still scared of the thing.

Weren't the rocksliders fighting the Spiders and Brothers, though? Joseph thought. Then again, there were human traitors working for the Spiders on this side. No doubt some rocksliders were traitors to their people as well.

This rockslider moved to the base of the arch. It reshaped itself, so that two wide bulbous extensions appeared from its sides. That explained how it had grabbed him. The quasi-arms extended to the sides of the arch where six conduits were stuck onto the outside of the arch. This was where all the power from the generators was going. The rockslider oozed the end of its arm over the tubing and then seemed to stiffen its flesh, holding the tubing and pulling it loose. From where he was, Joseph could make out that the ends of the tubes were colour coded, pink, blue and yellow, to the sockets in which they had been. When the conduits had all been pulled, the electrical energy around the arch died and the vision of the pipes running into the far wall vanished, like a TV picture going out. The pipes ended at the arch in mid-air and beyond that was just rock. The rockslider began sticking the conduits back in, but with the colours mismatched. When it was done, the electrical show around the arch grew much more intense.

The rockslider walked through the arch into the far room. This thing was a portal! Joseph realized. He needed to get out. He needed to tell Dasrath. Judging by the sulphur stink, it connected to Zolpash. The Brothers were using the hydropower to create a bridge back home, one that did not depend on the magical alignment of stars. The boxes around Joseph were probably meant to supply the Spiders. The pipes of water from the pool were for Zolpash too.

The electrical storm around the arch worsened. Tendrils of blue current arced out to the light bulbs closest to the arch and blow them apart. Joseph had seen enough James Bond movies to know what was happening. The rockslider had overloaded this thing so that it would self-destruct now that the army had found the generators.

The floor shook. The steel beams in the ceiling rattled. Joseph ran for the door but pressing the symbols there did nothing. He was going to die before he figured it out. A steel beam fell to the ground behind him and sent reverberations into his ankles. The air smelled like someone was burning chicken and the room flickered as lightning flashed around the arch.

Joseph saw no other doors in the room. The only other way in was through the water, if indeed it was connected to the water in the generator room. Joseph tossed his boots and socks aside, and stripped to his underwear. As he was about to plunge into the water, an electrical arc struck its surface. Joseph paused. It was the only one so far, but there was no telling if it would happen again. The arch's legs cracked, and black gas leaked out from within the metal. That could never be good, Joseph thought. He dove into the water and started swimming. He took a breath at the wall and pushed himself downward, looking for a way out under the surface. He found an opening in the wall and took it.

Even under water, the shocks of the collapsing portal knocked Joseph around. There was just enough light to see his hands as he swam. He kept telling himself to simply swim straight. He was sure to hit a wall and that would guide him in the right direction. After what felt like an age, he had not found a wall. Maybe he was going down not out? He thought about reversing direction.

Joseph's fingers hit solid rock. But it was ahead of him. Was it the left wall or the right wall?

In the end it didn't matter. He needed air. Even if the direction he picked led him back to the portal room. He ran his hands on the wall and kicked himself along. His chest was tight with the need for oxygen and the pungent sulphur taste of the water on his lips increased his urge to get air. His head kept bumping into rock above and he swam on. Then he found space. There was no air left in his lungs and he had almost no energy left to kick. With the last of his strength he made the last few feet upward and heaved a few open-mouthed breaths, clinging to the edge of the pool.

The lights were flickering in the shaking cavern and Joseph remembered threat of the lightning bolts arcing off the portal. He pulled himself up and out. He lay there breathing hard. For a moment, that was all he could do. More things fell from the ceiling and Joseph made himself get up, staggering to the corridor. The shaking ground made him bounce off the walls as he tried to remember the way out. Just as he felt he recognized the right direction, the lights failed.

He tried to keep a sense of which direction was out, but it soon failed and he was hitting walls and taking corners he was not sure led to the exit or even if they led anywhere at all. Lights hit him from the side and Sergeant Collins was there wielding the largest flashlight he had ever seen. She grabbed Joseph and pulled him back the way they had come, emerging into daylight.

"What's happening in there?" Dasrath asked with his notepad.

"Spiders set place to blow up. Run."

The workers and guards were already heading away on the road as the ground vibrated and rocked. Some of the soldiers were escorting them and Collins ran to join her subordinates. Joseph was still unsteady on his feet, but he ran after her. After only two step Dasrath grabbed his shoulder, turning him around. With a smile, the lieutenant pointed him at the helicopter, its rotors already spinning.

The two made their way to the helicopter but while Joseph scrambled in Dasrath stood watching the door to the tunnel building. Another building collapsed and the pilot was getting frantic, evidently screaming at Dasrath. Joseph climbed back out and pulled at the lieutenant who allowed himself to be pulled backwards, but kept his eyes on the entrance to the tunnel, even after the helicopter took off.

Lightning streaked from another building, arcing into the air and exploding the wooden structure. Cracks appeared in the ground as more lightning shot through. Even with the helicopter flying up and away, Joseph was waiting to be knocked out of the sky. They flew over the road, passing Collins' soldiers and the crowd of workers who were running away.

The sky flashed orange and the helicopter jerked as though hit in the back and then as if it was being pulled to earth by an anchor. It fell spinning, the green trees below filling the side window until the pilot found the right maneuver to stabilize them. They swung around to look at the camp, but it was gone. There was no waterfall, no building, no people. Instead, there was just a round bowl-shaped hole a half-mile across, its sides as smooth as glass.

~ ~ ~ ∶ ∶ ~ ∶ ~ ∶ ~ ∶ ∶ ~ ~ ~

When the helicopter landed at Army Headquarters, no one spoke or even looked at each other. A few military police came up to the helicopter and collected their guns and gear then marched them in a line to a detention area. Joseph and Dasrath got cells across the corridor from each other. Dasrath knew the guard well enough that he was allowed to have his pencils and notepad back. They passed messages to each other, tossing them through the iron-barred doors.

"What happened down there?" Dasrath wanted to know.

Joseph told him.

"You sure about the rockslider?"

Joseph nodded.

"Without evidence," Dasrath wrote, "No one believe us. That bad thing about losing workers."

"No. Bad thing is they died! Tragedy!"

Dasrath looked at him from across the corridor like Joseph was a complaining six-year-old. He wrote, "That they died is sad. Tragedy would be if they died and we can't fix things."

Joseph knew Dasrath was right. If they did not get help all of those people had died in vain and all of Mayali's effort had been for nothing at all. It was time to tell Dasrath the truth.

"I know someone," Joseph told him. "Helped us find Zarco. Anansi."

Dasrath shrugged. "Fairy tale won't help we."

"Anansi the Spider is real," Joseph wrote. "One of Spider gods." He told Dasrath as much as he could with as few words as possible.

The man seethed as he read, then scribbled a fast reply. "Keeping that information back was betrayal."

"I didn't trust you then. Trying to protect Mayali. Anansi helped us."

"You can't trust a Spider god," Dasrath wrote. "They hate us."

"Anansi is good." Joseph replied. Then he added a correction underneath. "She not evil at least. She not looking to kill us. Other Spiders her enemies."

Dasrath took some time to think after reading this, then thoughtfully wrote his response: "ALL Spiders our enemies." Then he sat in the far corner and ignored Joseph while he scratched at the wall with his pencil. Soon after, guards escorted Dasrath out. They brought him back after what was at least a couple of hours. Joseph pelted him with a note asking what had happened, but got no response.

Joseph was taken to an interrogation room soon after and left to sit alone, barefoot, on an unpainted wooden bench at a dark table with peeling varnish. A colonel carrying a clipboard entered. With him was Anansi, who was wearing a captain's uniform, her hair pulled back severely and tied. When he noticed her name tag, Joseph almost laughed. It said, 'Nancy R. Aspide.' She grinned back at him from under her cap.

"The simplest tricks are the best," she told him. *"Now, pretend you're a stupid boy who doesn't know anything and I'll get you out of here. That shouldn't be hard for you."*

As with Mayali, Joseph could follow the spoken conversation through Anansi's mind.

"I think you right," the colonel said. "He look like he lost. I sure Dasrath just pull he into this whole thing. That man gone crazy I think. All he can talk about is giant spider and that the boy here had to fight a monster make out of jelly. Poor child."

"But there was a rockslider. I didn't fight it, but—"

"Stay quiet," Anansi told Joseph. To the colonel she said, "I think the boy gon' be happy to done with this. He parents gon' be happy too. They in town ready to meet he and carry he back home."

The colonel signed a few sheets on the clipboard then handed the pen and papers to Joseph. It was just a formality, Joseph realized as he read it. That he agreed to return when requested and that he had not been mistreated while in custody and so on.

"Don't read. Just sign," Anansi said. *"I told you to look stupid."*

"Fine, I'll sign really slow."

There were four places to sign and Joseph did so, adding a little extra to the bottom of each page as he pretended that writing was difficult.

Joseph handed the clipboard back and Anansi lifted him up by the elbow as the colonel checked that he had signed correctly. As they were about to go through the door, the colonel called them back.

"Wait," the man said. Joseph tensed waiting to see what was wrong. The colonel walked up to Joseph and extended his hand for a shake. Joseph saw the serious expression on the colonel's face. He noted the man's name for the first time. It was Franklyn, Dasrath's friend from the e-mails. Joseph gave a slight nod and took the colonel's hand, shook it firmly and left with Anansi.

As they walked down the corridor alone, Anansi asked, *"What was with all that eye contact between you and the colonel?"*

"I don't know. Maybe he just has a lot of respect for me?"

Anansi laughed. But Joseph knew the real reason. Franklyn had been trying to judge how trustworthy Joseph was after seeing what the boy had written on the bottom of every page on the clipboard in large letters: "BELIEVE DASRATH!!!"

~ ~ ~ ∷ ~ ∶ ~ ∷ ~ ~ ~

Anansi took them home driving one of her taxis. In the side mirror, Joseph watched the helicopter on the landing pad as they pulled out of the main gate and were soon speeding down the East Coast highway.

"Mayali is leaving for Suriname this afternoon," Anansi said,

handing him a box with running shoes inside. *"You'll be able to say good-bye to her before she goes and you can meet your parents this afternoon."*

"Mayali's leaving?"

"Yes."

"Is she okay?" Joseph asked. He examined the shoes. Black with thick soles. Strong stitching. He hoped he kept these shoes for a longer time than usual. *"What about Zarco and her father and—"*

"She's fine. Zarco won't be able to touch her when she leaves and that's the most important thing. She was telling me earlier about how Rafeek had found her father, but that's just her being nervous about going away. Once she gets out of the country, she'll see that she needs to just find a quiet life to live and she'll be happy."

"A quiet life?" Joseph teased. *"Like you?"*

"I would have a very quiet life right now if it wasn't for the two of you."

When they arrived at the Hiladora factory, Joseph was relieved to see the familiar building. *"Oh, Tara has been living here all week."* Anansi said as they were getting out of the car.

"And you're only telling me now?"

"That's why it's called a surprise. I'm sending you, her and your parents back to Mabaruma tomorrow on a plane. Unless you want to stay. I could use a man like you in my operation. A man who knows the right time to play stupid."

Joseph ignored the job offer and ran up to the hotel rooms in his perfectly fitted shoes. He found Tara watching a movie on the couch and she jumped up, happy to see him. They hugged and kissed. She smelled so good, as always. And felt good too.

He disentangled before he got carried away, looking warily around for Mayali who would tease him. He took his notepad out and wrote, "Mayali?"

Tara gave him an annoyed look and pointed to herself and

her body speaking words Joseph was sure amounted to "I'm your girlfriend, you're supposed to ask about me."

He gave her a come-on-be-serious look and pointed to the note.

Tara wrote, "Gone look for father."

"Where?"

"Water place Zarco have. Rafeek with her."

"You didn't go?" Joseph asked.

"Rafeek said Mayali want me wait for you."

"How long ago?"

"One hour," Tara wrote, then shrugged that she was unsure.

"She planning to fight Zarco?"

"Just gone to look."

Joseph laughed. Mayali would never go to just look. He had to go stop her before she tried to invade the place. But how?

Sirens blasted the air from the road. When they stepped out onto their third floor balcony, they saw army and police vehicles speed into the factory compound, surrounding the building. No one was coming to the hotel. The fence had fooled them into thinking it was separate.

Colonel Franklyn was in the lead. Lieutenant Dasrath was in the backseat of one of the open-top jeeps, handcuffed to the roll bar. His eyes caught Joseph's. They stared at each other for a while, Dasrath's face twisted with anger.

Joseph decided it would take too long to sort this out with the army. He needed to stop Mayali from doing something dangerous. He signalled to Tara and the two of them headed out the door. When they ran for the road, Joseph could see Dasrath calling to the soldiers, but they were too far away, raiding the factory.

Joseph and Tara got into a minibus calmly, trying to look as much as they could like an ordinary teenaged couple. The bus ran the 44 route which took them straight down Vlissingen Road to the corner of Church Street.

"Mayali?" Joseph called when he got out.

There was no reply. They walked into the parking lot and were immediately surrounded by eight security guards who rushed out from doors on either side. The uniforms flickered and Joseph caught a glimpse of the Brothers underneath the illusion. He could probably still find a way to get free if he ran, but Tara would be left behind. He stood with his hands up to let himself be taken.

Tara lifted her knee high and kicked her heel into the crotch of the nearest Brother. It made him squeal and gasp and Tara ran past him. Two others ran after her. Joseph tried to follow, but the remaining six Brothers grabbed him. He tried to force them off, grabbing at their clothes. He pulled one by the hood of the robe and it came off, showing Joseph the head of a Brother for the first time. The man's head was bald and gaunt, with a full beard. He had eight eyes; two large unblinking ones in the normal place, with two outside those and four in a bent row above. The sight shocked Joseph long enough for the other Brothers to get a firm hold on him. The last one put his hood back in place and they carried Joseph away.

CHAPTER 16
Search and Rescue

The first thing Mayali thought was that she had to coordinate with Rafeek to free Chloe. But Rafeek stood still at Zarco's side, head down. The big man saw her look at the boy and laughed. "You think you lil rat friend here gon' help you? Who you think tell he to bring you here?"

"Rafeek?" Mayali looked at him.

"This boy only got one friend. A white, powdery friend. Not so, boy?"

Rafeek looked up at Zarco and mumbled, "I do what you tell me."

"And now you want your medicine, eh?"

"Stupid junkie," said Percy, shaking his head. Mayali noticed her knife clipped to his waistband.

The boy kept his eyes down. "Please. I do what you tell me."

"Yes, you even bring the dog, like I say." Zarco had one of the men take Rafeek out a side door. The man turned to Mayali. "You shouldn't have take me dog. That dog is fo' me to deal with. I decide what happen to she and now I gon' decide something bad. I think—"

Mayali had been eyeing the third door in the room and now she sprang for it, lifting the heavy latch. The Brothers were not fast enough and she got it open, only to find a storeroom. As the men laughed behind her she noticed it was filled with the belongings of the prisoners. She scanned past the shoes and shirts and saw Jamesy's duffel bag with his gun case on top of the pile. She reached for the gun although she had little idea how to use it, or even if it was loaded, but strong hands grabbed her and pulled her back into the room. Zarco walked up and stroked her under the chin.

"Too bad I don't actually know nothing about you father. I would want talk to he about you behaviour. You's a botheration pickney and nothing good ever come from—"

Jamesy pounced. He was breathing hard as he rushed Zarco and pushed him into the storeroom, sending the large man sprawling onto the floor. With a last effort before the Brothers grabbed him, Jamesy slammed the latch closed. The other prisoners manoeuvred to obstruct the Brothers trying to catch Mayali.

Mayali used the confusion to grab her knife from Percy's waist. She flicked open the blade and brought it down into the back of his knee. He howled and collapsed, distracting the Brothers more. When Mayali ripped the knife free with a twist, he howled again.

There were still two guards near the main door, so Mayali ran out of the side door where Rafeek had been led. It led her onto a railed catwalk, high over the darker part of the giant room she had glimpsed earlier. She ran to where the catwalk passed through some shadows and found the mouth of a large pipe. It was open at the other end and led to the middle of the room along the ceiling. With nothing but open space around her, she climbed in and scrambled through on all fours. The pipe let her out at another catwalk. Rolls of electrical wire and cartons of fluorescent light tubes were piled all around. There was the smell of sulphur everywhere. The smell of home.

From up there, Mayali had a clear view of the room's layout. Construction was focused on the far end, with Brothers welding and hammering. That was where most of the lights were. This end of the room was not in use, though it seemed that the construction was mostly done. She suspected that when the work was over, there would be light bulbs everywhere, but for now, a useful darkness prevailed.

Below, in the centre of the floor, an arch of sparking black metal stood on a platform, as wide as a football goal. A tall metal fence surrounded the arch. Behind her, she could hear Brother Hakk's voice. He was leading Chloe out of the prison room by one of the long sticks and calling for help from those on the floor. A few of them came towards him, climbing stairs to get up to their level. They did not go into the prison room, however. The fight in there must have been over. Instead, the Brothers spread through the gangways and catwalks and empty floors, shining flashlights into the dark, where Mayali might be.

They would find her if she stayed where she was. Mayali looked towards the far end. More large pipes and steel bars were stored that way on platforms near the side wall. She climbed down a dark flight of stairs, carrying a roll of the slimmest wire she could find. The pipes were held by nylon straps, stronger and stretchier than rope or wire, but easier to cut. She used her knife to cut all but a few. Those she frayed and tied with her wire.

The swaying torch beams were getting closer.

Mayali tossed the other end of the wire over the platform rail to the ground. She walked to the floor. Using the strapping fabric, she padded her hands then got a good grip on the coiled end of the wire. She moved as far as the wire would let her, passing the arch and wondering what it was. When the wire went taut, Mayali leaned back and pulled. The weakened straps above gave way and the steel pipes and beams rolled, toppling down in a ringing cacophony.

Mayali ran towards the dark end of the room. Above, she could see Brother Hakk by the prison room with Chloe. Following Hakk's commands, the others ran along the catwalks towards the place from which the pipes had fallen. This cleared the way back to the prison room and she climbed the stairs back up. Hakk could sense her, from the buzz of the Spider's Touch, but he kept looking for her on the lower levels.

She kept to the shadows while she approached Hakk. When she was close enough, she barked at him as she jumped out of the shadows. He was startled enough for her to close the distance between them, and she knocked Chloe's control stick out of his hand.

The dog launched herself at him. He barely dodged, then leaped over the side rail, tumbling to a platform below and crying out in pain. Mayali unstrapped Chloe and ran back into the prison room. It was empty. The storeroom was latched and Mayali wondered if Zarco was still in there. She decided not to find out and ran out the main door and up the stairs, into sunlight.

Mayali and Chloe dashed around the corner and ran through the parking lot. A crowd had formed at the road. Father Garcia, Jamesy and the other prisoners were there with the Brothers trying to recapture them. Bystanders however had intervened, saving them. The Brothers were trying to project the illusion that they were police, but there were just too many people giving them close scrutiny for their power to be that effective. The crowd knew something was wrong.

The phone in Mayali's pocket buzzed. It was a message. "Mayali, this is Joseph. I'm trapped in a room at the water plant."

Mayali replied, "Zarco u cant fool me."

"Found phone on the floor after they lock me in the store room. Heard Brothers say u were loose b4 they left."

Zarco had hit the ground hard when Jamesy pushed him, Mayali remembered. The phone could have fallen out. "Tell me abt room," Mayali asked.

"I don't know where it is exactly."

"Wht inside?"

Joseph wrote, "Shoes. Jamesy's gun and bag."

The police had showed up at the road and Tara was talking to them, pointing at the Brothers. The Brothers would have to come back soon and then Joseph might get hurt, if it really was him.

Mayali texted, "Dont use touch. Dey hear." Telling Chloe to follow, she ran back to the entrance and down the three flights of stairs. Chloe barked at the store room door and wagged her snub tail.

"Joseph?" Mayali called. Then she remembered he couldn't hear. She texted him. "At d door. Hit 3 time."

After a few seconds there came three knocks. She lifted the latch to the door and found Joseph crouched against the wall with the gun in his hands. He got out holding his left ribs. Footsteps sounded on the metal stairs above. Mayali indicated to Joseph to move quietly and took him out to the catwalk. This tactic had worked before, so she would try it again.

Except that Zarco was coming toward the door from one end of the catwalk. He was talking to a few Brothers and his head was turned. Mayali signalled Joseph to follow her. They crept the other way and down a flight of stairs. She remembered that there was a maze of pipes and barrels on a dark side floor here.

A message came into her phone, vibrating it. "I know that thing," said the text from Joseph. He pointed down at the arch on the floor.

"Wat?" she texted back, glancing over to where she had last seen Zarco.

"Take you to Zolpash."

A movement in the corner of the room closest to them caught their eye. It was Rafeek. He had his arms wrapped around his knees and he was shaking.

"You!" said Mayali, keeping her voice low, as she walked over to him. They needed to get going, but first she needed Rafeek to explain himself to her. "How you can do that to we? You was we friend."

"Sorry," said Rafeek, not looking up.

"You can't just sorry. We treat you good and you gone and act like a real junkie. I should have know from the start, but you fool we, make we think that you really want help we—"

"I not no junkie." said Rafeek, his eyes wet.

"Yeah?" asked Mayali "And this is what?" She twisted his wrist, revealing the pipe in his hand. There was nothing in it. He had not yet gotten his drug payment in all the confusion.

"I stop all that," he said. "When I meet you and Joseph I did stop. I didn't do none of that." Rafeek looked up at her. "Zarco catch me that night at the radio station. Every day he get me high and he make me can't do without it. And then he say if I want more I had to bring you." Rafeek, held Mayali's hand. "He never say he did going to hurt you. I didn't know."

Mayali threw his hand off. "You know, yes."

Rafeek looked down, shaking his head.

The phone buzzed. Joseph wanted them to get moving.

"You can't tell me you didn't know. Look at me. Tell me the truth. You didn't know?"

"Yes," Rafeek admitted. "But I feel like I did going to dead. I had to do it."

"You didn't had to do nothing. You—"

Chloe growled and snarled.

A pair of pit bulls came up the stairway. That was the only exit Mayali knew of. The dogs stalked them as a team, circling and coming at Mayali and Joseph. Every time the dogs tried to attack, however, Chloe got in their way barking and driving them back. Mayali could tell this was a losing battle, though. The dogs were coming from different directions and would soon tire Chloe out. Plus their noise was going to draw the Brothers.

She looked around for something to assist her. She had the knife, but that meant putting her arms far too close to the dogs' giant teeth. No pipes or steel rods were on the floor, nothing that could be used as a weapon. Rafeek had balled himself up in the corner.

Joseph screamed in Mayali's mind. One of the dogs had bitten him in the calf. Chloe used that chance to clamp down on the dog's neck. The second dog attacked.

"*Run,*" Mayali said, pulling Joseph towards the stairs.

"*But Chloe.*"

"*You stay here, you'll die. She's saving us. Come on.*"

They scrambled down the stairs, the other dog chasing, but having a hard time attacking as they went down the incline. When they got to the floor, however, the dog was on them. It snarled and lunged at Mayali, but Joseph tumbled a barrel in its way. That did not hurt the dog, but distracted it enough that they got away.

Lights were shining on them now as the Brothers converged from all around, flashlights in hand. Brother Hakk, in his red robe, was coming from the construction area, his distinct rasping voice giving orders. Zarco was coming down the stairs from the catwalk above. Some of the construction crew pivoted the floodlights towards them. There was nowhere to hide. But the light showed Mayali a crowbar lying on a crate. She swung it in a full arc toward the dog, hitting its shoulder. The dog howled and jumped away, but it was a hardened attack dog. It came back at them. Mayali hit it a few more times and it kept its distance, looking for a new way in.

With the Brothers coming at them, Joseph pulled Mayali to follow him. They were running blind, just trying to get away with no plan. At least Mayali was. Joseph seemed to have an idea. He led her through the gates to the fenced area of the arch and onto the platform. The reality of what Joseph had told her set in. Through the legs of the arch she could see the world of Zolpash. There were small cloudfires near the mountains in the distance and the sparkle of morning sun off the curving lattice of hardwater roads.

And Spiders. The monstrous shape of a few could be seen in the distance, near a landship.

"We can't go to Zolpash," Mayali said.

"I'm not planning to."

"What then?"

Joseph smiled.

Brother Hakk and Zarco entered the enclosure. A dozen brothers entered behind them.

"Nowhere to run but to the land of the gods themselves," said Brother Hakk. *"If you are humble, they may even forgive you."*

Zarco pulled a gun from his waist. *"Forget speeches, Hakk."* He walked towards them, aiming at Mayali.

"Stop!" said Joseph. *"If you want to live, you better start running the other way."*

Mayali turned to see that Joseph manipulating the cables of the portal. The arch was crackling wildly with electrical sparks.

"What did you do?" Zarco asked.

"A trick I learned this morning. Overloaded one of your other portals and blew it up. Left a hole a mile wide. That one was a lot bigger, but I bet this one still kills all of you if you stick around."

Brother Hakk said, *"But we don't have—"*

Zarco yelled at Joseph, *"We'll just switch the cables back after I shoot you."*

"Won't work," said Joseph. *"It's already overloaded. It's going to explode no matter what now."* Mayali had known Joseph long enough to tell that the last part was a lie. She hoped he was convincing enough to fool the Brothers. A lightning bolt sizzled out from the arch and struck the ground near Zarco. Joseph added, *"You're welcome to stay and try stopping it if you want, but the sooner you start running, the safer you'll be."*

Zarco muttered a curse, turned and began jogging back to the exit of the building. Most of the Brothers followed. Brother Hakk and three of his followers stayed, however. At his signal, one of them bolted the gate.

"What?" said Mayali. *"You don't believe this thing is really going to blow up? You're going to die if you stay here!"*

"I absolutely believe you," Brother Hakk said. *"I welcome death. We shall stay here to ensure the enemies of the gods perish and the gods shall reward us in the afterlife."*

CHAPTER 17
Death of a Portal

Joseph felt a chunk of the ceiling fall nearby. He saw one of the upper floors buckle, spilling pipes and tubes and steel everywhere. Brother Hakk and his men just stood still, waiting for the end. An instinct in Joseph had him say, "Our Father, who art in heaven ..." He faltered unsure whether those words had enough power to save him.

The phone rumbled in Joseph's hand. "You go right, I'll go left," said the message. He looked over and Mayali nodded slightly. They ran, Mayali with her knife drawn.

Brother Hakk went after Mayali. Two other Brothers came for Joseph. He ducked under one's arm but the other Brother tackled him at the waist and drove him to the ground. His head hit the concrete hard and his vision flashed white. He shook his head clear just in time to see Mayali's knife spinning along the concrete towards the Brother at the gate. Brother Hakk had both her wrists pinned in his furry Spider-fingers. Mayali bit him through his robe, but he did not seem to notice.

There was an angry cry from behind Brother Hakk and Joseph caught sight of Rafeek leaping off the top of the fence and landing on the man's shoulders. He wrapped his arms and legs about the man, twisting and dragging him to the ground with Mayali's help.

The Brothers wrangling with Joseph got up to help their leader and Joseph sprang to his feet and ran for the knife. The last Brother, the one guarding the gate, saw him and raced him for the blade. The man dove and grasped it ahead of Joseph, but that was the plan. Joseph ignored him and ran for the gate instead. Before the man even realized he had been tricked, Joseph had the gate open.

"Mayali, come," he shouted.

She turned to where Brother Hakk was just getting up from the floor. Two Brothers were playing hide-and-seek with Rafeek around the arch, but the Brother with the knife was coming for Mayali. She kicked at Brother Hakk.

"This place will blow up any time now!"

Rafeek ran by and pulled her, the Brothers chasing all three of them into the open floor. Joseph saw Chloe ahead. She was fighting one of the big dogs. The other lay bleeding to the side, one front leg broken.

With Rafeek's help, they held the gate shut as the Brothers charged it from the other side.

"Joseph set that thing to blow up?" Refeek asked.

"Yes, as long as them cable plug in the wrong way."

He swallowed and took a breath. The door shook with another charge from the Brothers. He said, "You two go. I gon' keep them busy so they can't change the cable."

"What? No!" Mayali pulled at his arm. "Come with we."

More Brothers were running from the construction area. Another was climbing the gate from inside. Joseph could hear Hakk commanding his men to kill them.

"Let's go," Joseph told her. *"We don't have time. It won't change anything if you die with him."*

"Come!" she said to Rafeek.

He shook his head.

With a grunt of frustration, Mayali turned and ran with Joseph for the stairs. Already escape was unlikely and Joseph braced himself for a fight.

A loud crack echoed up and down the chamber. The dog fighting Chloe fell to the ground. Near the exit, Lieutenant Dasrath was kneeling with Jamesy's rifle. He fired another shot and Joseph felt it fly over their heads at the Brothers chasing them.

They did not look back, but continued to run as some of the

Brothers fired their own guns at Dasrath. Mayali ran in front, Chloe at Joseph's side. They raced up the stairs toward Dasrath.

The climb was almost impossible with the shaking of the stairway. Joseph had to lift Chloe over his shoulders and that made it even harder to balance. Around them the room was sparking as wires tore loose and pieces of the walls were breaking off.

When they reached Dasrath at the top, Mayali said, "Thanks. I rea—" She stopped short, looking back at the arch. Rafeek was still down there, using Mayali's knife to hold off Hakk and another Brother who were trying to disconnect the power cables. A giant Spider was reaching its head through to try and bite him, though it was too large to walk through the arch.

"Shoot them," Mayali said to the soldier.

"No more bullets," he replied.

Mayali turned to go back down. Joseph stopped her with an arm around her chest.

"That thing is going to blow up before you get there. We have to go," he said.

She took a last look at Rafeek down below then glared at Joseph and ran for the surface. Dasrath followed them through the prison room and up the stairs. They broke into the daylight and ran through the parking lot. Police and army officers were everywhere.

"Mayali, it's not safe for them here. This explosion is going to be huge."

She said to Dasrath, "You got fo' get everybody far away. This thing gon' blow up big."

It helped that the soldiers followed Dasrath's orders. It helped even more that Mayali, Chloe and Joseph, their faces dirty and terrified ran straight past the crowd without looking around. People got the idea and joined their escape.

Dasrath split off, organising his troops to complete the evacuation.

A slow rumbling sound began from under the ground and the

crowd screamed. People were fleeing their buildings and joining the panic.

"*Are we far away enough yet?*" Mayali asked as they kept running.

"*I don't know,*" Joseph said. "*I only had this happen to me once before. I don't know how it works.*"

When they were about a block away, moving east alongside the canal, they heard a loud 'whump' and then silence. In unison, the crowd stopped and looked back. Dust was rising from the center of the water plant compound, but the buildings were intact.

Joseph said, "*I guess this one wasn't as big as—*"

A breaking noise flew to them along the ground and the largest building tumbled over, its blue roof tilting and falling through the ground. Joseph realized that the destruction caused by the overloading of the arch had barely penetrated to the top, but it had undermined the entire complex. Starting in the center, the buildings sank and fell into the pit.

"*Rafeek ...*" Mayali said as she looked back at the imploded water complex, dust still rising from its carcass. She could not complete the thought.

Rafeek had chosen a fate that confounded Joseph's understanding. Did he care about anything in the world enough to die for it?

"*Mayali,*" he said. "*I don't know anymore if Heaven is a real place. But if it is, it's for people like Rafeek. He's not—*"

She wasn't listening. Mayali was looking down the road, her face stiff, except for an angry twisting at one corner of her mouth. "*Go find Dasrath,*" she said.

"*What?*"

"*Zarco.*"

CHAPTER 18

Rocks and Hard Places

Despite his bulk and tattoos, Zarco blended in well with the crowd of confused people talking on their phones half a block from them. He was watching the action at the water plant with his blue shades still on. Mayali balled her hands into fists, wishing she still had her knife.

Joseph pointed back to the explosion, *"I can't find Dasrath in that."*

While hundreds had fled the destruction, thousands had come to see it for themselves. The scattered police and soldiers could barely be seen as the crowd pressed to the edge of the site.

"The soldiers will find him for you on their radios," said Mayali. *"I'll keep an eye on Zarco."*

Chloe whimpered when Joseph turned.

"You stay," Mayali told her. The dog sat and watched as Joseph ran toward the wreckage.

Left alone, Mayali thought about Rafeek and the hopeful way he had looked at her when he told her to run. Had he been trying to save her or himself?

The crowd was thinning out here as more people went back to the water plant for a look. She couldn't use it to hide anymore. That fence would—

Zarco stiffened. Then he smiled. *"You think you won, girl?"* he said to her, his voice whisper-like in her mind. *"As long as I'm walking free you'll have no peace. I'll find you again."* He turned and ran, showing speed for a man his size.

There were two things Mayali was certain of in that moment. The first was that she could not win a fight with Zarco. He was too strong and she had no weapon left. Plus every fight in her life had been a delaying tactic to escape. She had never actually beaten anyone.

The other certainty was that she had to stop Zarco now or he would be her death. So she chased him, dodging through the bystanders and gaining speed as she worked her way toward the empty road. Chloe ran ahead of her.

On one side was the long, straight path of the Lama Canal, its waters unusually turbulent. To the other, the industrial buildings were soon replaced by overgrown empty lots and construction sites. The street itself ended at a dead end. The only way out was a bridge and pump house leading across the canal into the semi-jungle of the Botanical Gardens.

Mayali would never find Zarco if he got to the trees. *"Get him,"* she said to the dog who was already far ahead. Chloe sped up.

Zarco glanced back as Chloe gained on him. Without stopping, he pulled his gun and fired at the running dog. Three bullets sparked on the roadway before Chloe leapt up and snapped her jaws around his wrist.

He cried out as the dog twisted him around and the gun went flying into the dark waters of the canal. The flow in the canal was brisk and noisy now. The explosion must have ruptured it downstream, pulling the water that way.

Zarco flung the dog off, grunting when her teeth scraped free. Blood splattered from his hand to the ground as he ran. He made it onto the bridge, Chloe at his heels. She got a good grip on his ankle and he stumbled, catching himself on the crude railing outside of the pump station, above the middle of the canal. He seemed more afraid of the water than the dog.

With his heavy boot he stomped Chloe's back. She growled and yanked his ankle to one side causing him to slip again. His sunshades fell into the water and Mayali could see fear in his eyes as he twisted away from the water.

She was almost at the entrance of the bridge. Zarco locked eyes with her and she smiled. He gritted his teeth, heaved his boot back and swung a kick into Chloe's ribs. It knocked the dog through one of the wide spaces in the railing and she fell into the water, floating away in the current, struggling for the shore.

Mayali tried to turn back, but she was too close. Zarco grabbed her neck. Before he could get a firm grip, she reached up with both hands and pried him off.

She had ended up at the end of the short railing, between Zarco and the safety of the Gardens. This was not her kind of fight. The man was just going to ram through her.

She let him come. When he shaped his shoulder at her chest, she dodged to the outside of the rail and grabbed his elbow with both her arms, using his momentum to swing him around the corner of the rail, right off the bridge.

They tumbled into the water together, Mayali breathing deep before they hit. This rushing dark water was nothing like the calm pool where Rafeek had taught her the basics of swimming, but she knew Zarco would be afraid and clueless in water.

At first, he struggled wildly, ignoring Mayali as he fought against the water. Holding her breath, she reached around the struggling body of the big man. She shifted to his back and locked one arm around his neck, his beard scratchy even under water. With her other hand she pulled her hold tighter. She could keep this up until he lost consciousness and then pull him to the bank.

Being strangled got his attention. He reached up and pulled her hair, wrenching her neck painfully to the side. The message was clear – he would make sure they died together unless she let him go. Already her lungs hurt from the effort of keeping in its air.

She kept her chokehold, fighting against the slackening of her muscles and the faintness in her head.

Her feet scraped bottom. The water was draining from the canal and the level had fallen. Zarco sensed this too and he dumped her off his shoulders using the canal floor for leverage. He took heavy, howling breaths as he staggered around. She wondered if she could not simply hold him under the water in his weakened state, but he had the idea first. He half jumped, half collapsed in her direction and used his weight to pin her.

Water rushed into her nose as he knocked the breath out of her. She squirmed as he grabbed for her throat, unable to get out from under him. When she kicked at him, the water kept her from putting any force into it.

Mayali bent toward the wrist Chloe had bitten earlier and got hold of it. She bit at the already torn flesh and Zarco jerked it away. This took the fight out of him. He rose and started wading out. He could not kill her, so he was escaping.

Neither of them could walk a straight line as Mayali followed him out of the water and onto the road in a panting, slow motion chase that made her chuckle wryly at its comicality.

Zarco fell to all fours in one of the construction sites, vomiting water. He rose to his knees and wiped his mouth, getting his breath back. Except for the wrist, he was not injured Mayali saw. She could not beat him and soon she would not be able to stop him from getting away. Joseph was back at the plant with the crowd. Chloe had been swept away. Rafeek was dead. The canal was down to a trickle.

She looked at the mounds of sand, stone and boulders near her as she walked into the construction area. She picked up a vaguely egg-shaped chunk of granite the size of her head. Her fingers ached from keeping her grip on it. Panicked, Zarco started crawling away in the grass. She followed. Mayali aimed and brought the rock down on his right ankle as she collapsed from the effort.

There was a clear, snapping sound and Zarco screamed, loud for a half-drowned man. But he kept crawling, his injured foot dragging at a twisted angle. He could still escape on one foot. Once he got his breath back, he'd still be more than a match for her. Mayali stood shakily, the rock in her hands again.

She closed the distance, noting the bulging wetness of Zarco's neck. Mayali positioned the most jagged edge of the stone to strike. She could end this game now and kill him. Rafeek's gap-toothed grin flashed in her mind. She could have revenge.

This time, Mayali brought the rock down even harder, right onto the other ankle. Again she heard the snap and again he screamed. But this time he stopped crawling, merely sobbing as he rolled side to side.

Revenge wasn't why she had come to this place.

Zarco wasn't the only enemy. And the fight didn't end with him. Now he was a book full of secrets for the people of Earth to study. The Spiders would not catch them unprepared, and Jalana would have her allies. Mayali had kept her promise.

~ ~ ~ ∷ ~ ∶ ~ ∷ ~ ~ ~

Eventually Dasrath showed up, Chloe and Joseph at his side. Malayi was glad to see the dog, happy that it had made it out of the canal. Dasrath took Zarco prisoner and left in a jeep.

Mayali wandered the outskirts of the wreckage with Chloe and Joseph, watching the police sort through the mess. Everyone in the buildings had run when the shaking started and Rafeek and the Brothers had been far too deep to be found. The water from the Lama canal had flowed in to fill the entire site, stopping all attempts to investigate.

"Well, this is an almighty mess," said Anansi, walking up behind Joseph and Mayali. *"I assume it's all your doing?"*

Joseph and Mayali hadn't even seen when Anansi had arrived and they were too traumatised to tolerate her humour. When she saw their expressions, she dropped it. *"Alright, come with me,"* she told them.

"Why?" Joseph asked.

"Because you killed the Brothers' portal and they're going to want revenge. You need to leave before they know you were here."

They walked to Anansi's car, looking over the destruction. "This gon' take some serious work to fix," Anansi noted. "The whole town gon' be without water fo' at least a couple week. And that is if they fly in emergency pump and stuff." She lifted her eyebrows in amusement and added, "Gon' be a big contract to repair all this. I should try and get the work for Hiladora Steel."

EPILOGUE 1

The next dawn at Ogle Airstrip, Joseph faced Mayali, saying goodbye. Anansi stood to the side, giving them some privacy. Joseph's parents and Tara were waiting in the plane while its propellers spun.

"I hope you find your father," he told her, then gave her a peck on the cheek. He smiled when she wiped at the spot with an annoyed grimace. Only after he was halfway to the plane did she finally reply.

"Joseph, thanks for helping me."

"You welcome."

Given the drama of his previous helicopter flights, the take-off seemed calm and relaxing. They climbed into the air and he looked east, Tara peering over his shoulder. The road ran along the coast into the distance disappearing under the rising sun. Soon Mayali would be in a car going that way, to yet another land. He wondered if there could ever be a place she called home.

The plane banked west, giving them a view of Georgetown laid out below. He and Tara leaned towards the other window to see, his nose right behind her. She was definitely the best-smelling person he knew. Below, he could see the main roads, the green swath of the Botanical Gardens, the Stabroek clock tower and the ships in the harbour. He felt not a sense of loss but of ownership. This was not good-bye.

Tara squeezed his hand and he smiled at her.

EPILOGUE 2

In a place between worlds, Anansi stood in her true form, taking up half the room. From the other side the rocksliders' leader approached through the portal.

"Must you insist on these face-to-face meetings?" Anansi asked. *"Or face-to-whatever it is you have. I'm not exactly full of leisure on the other side."*

Jalana had no sense of humour as usual. If a blob of jelly could frown, she was frowning. Anansi wondered if it was a feature of her race or just her individual personality. Since Jalana was the only rockslider she knew with the Spider's Touch, Anansi had never spoken to another. Jalana said, *"My people need water. It may have been my decision to destroy the portal, but its loss is your failure. I need your assurance that you'll re-establish a supply of water. No excuses. No messages through your vassals."*

A 'vassal' was exactly how Anansi viewed Jalana, but she let the rockslider continue the illusion of being an equal, replying in respectful tones. *"I apologize for that, Jalana. This inconveniences me as well. I have plans too that—"*

"Serpents take your plans! I have people depending on me to survive and I'm fighting a war. It cost me a great deal to have that girl sent over like you wanted, but I did it, because I have honour."

Always with the honour talk. Anansi had never understood the concept. She knew the definitions of it, of course, knew the limits it imposed, but she could not imagine why a being of sound mind would let themselves be chained to it. It was impossible for even its most ardent proponents to follow in any case.

"You have no honour," said Anansi.

"Still your tongue, Spider, or I—"

"I state fact. You tried to have the girl contact the human authorities and have them come aid you. That's not the pact we have."

" If I wait on you, my children's children will die slaves."

"Because of that I had the Guyana Army on my front lawn. I had to call in presidential favours to get that sorted out. And I mean Oval Office presidential, not the—"

"Your human affairs bore me. When shall I have my water?"

"I've constructed a total of four other portals," said Anansi. "All of them will be working by year's end. What happened with the equipment from Amaila? Is any of it salvageable?"

"The effects of the overloading were far from destructive. It actually created a bubble on the other side and brought everything back to Zolpash intact. Some of the workers were injured, but they all survived. And the arch itself seems damaged, but it's not destroyed."

"The workers survived too?"

"Yes," said Jalana. "And when you identify your next site, I will send them and the repaired arch over to set it up."

"Good" said Anansi. "The only problem is that you have a traitor on your side."

"Never," said Jalana, her anger shaking her body in waves.

"Never? Then how did the Brothers get my design? The portal they built in Georgetown had the exact power couplings as mine. Even the colours on the ends were the same. The boy was able to overload theirs the same way he saw you overload ours."

Jalana shifted her body in a way Anansi knew meant reluctant acceptance. "I will investigate. I give you my word of honour."

As she watched the rockslider leave, Anansi thought about Mayali. There was power in that girl's defiant soul. Magic that Anansi had planted there years before, but which was still a surprise in its flowering potency. What Mayali had become – what she could become! She needed to be watched and guided, and kept safe in a hidden place. When the war with Arachne came, Mayali would be a powerful weapon for Anansi.

EPILOGUE 3

The ferry sailed out onto the river as Mayali watched from the dock. The water stretched almost to the horizon before the far shore appeared. She remembered Joseph telling her that the entire river belonged to Suriname and she had laughed at the idea that anyone could own something so vast.

Joseph was back in his old life by now. Tara too. That was best. If Rafeek was any example, Mayali did not br ing fortune to anyone.

The ship blew a blast of its horn. She had spent an hour on it waiting to leave. The deck and walls had been clean. The engine had run almost silent. It had been three generations of improvement over *Lady Northcote*. But it had felt like a coffin around her. Anansi's plan, to send her to Holland, would set Mayali working for something she was not sure she wanted. She needed to be on her own.

Or almost on her own.

She slung her bag over her shoulder and patted the one-eyed, blue-grey dog on her head. Then Mayali turned her back on the water and walked up the muddy road, wondering where it led.

~ ~ ~ ∷ ~ ∶ ~ ∷ ~ ~ ~

About the Author

Imam Baksh is a writer from Guyana. He enjoys tales of magic, monsters and heroes of all kinds. He's also interested in history and how the world works, and never accepts any claim unless he's given proof. He enjoys research, which helps him write better stories and win many arguments (in fact, he hasn't lost an argument since June 1998).

As a boy, Imam left his countryside home on the Essequibo Coast to attend high school (Queens College) in the city of Georgetown, where he learned most of his bad habits. He became a trained teacher, specialized in English, but he had the most fun teaching physics because he got to use electricity on his students. These days he is a full-time writer and his short stories have won the Henry Josiah Prize for Children's Stories three times between 2006 and 2010.

His debut novel, **Children of the Spider**, won the 2015 Burt Award for Caribbean Literature.

TALES FOR YOUNG ADULTS
FROM BLOUSE & SKIRT BOOKS

ALL OVER AGAIN
BY A-DZIKO SIMBA GEGELE
Who Knew Growing up
Could be so Hard?

GROWING UP IS HARD. You know this. And when your mother has X-ray eyes and dances like a wobbling bag of water? When your father's idea of fun is to put all your money in a savings account and make you get up at 5 am every Sunday morning? When Kenny, Percival Thorton High's big show-off, is after Christina Parker - your Christina Parker? And when you have a shrimp of a little sister who is the bawlingest little six year old girl in the whole of Riverland? Then growing up is something you not sure you can manage at all. Who in their right mind could? Who? You?

All Over Again is an enchanting slice of boyhood. It is a charming coming of age story with a bold narrative style that pulls you into it.

Winner of the 2014 Burt Award for Caribbean Literature and longlisted for the 2015 International IMPAC Dublin Literary Award.

TALES FOR YOUNG ADULTS
FROM BLOUSE & SKIRT BOOKS

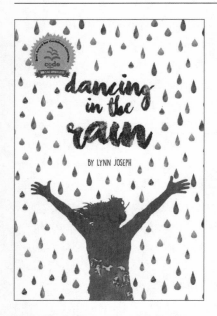

DANCING IN THE RAIN
BY LYNN JOSEPH
Finding Joy in the Small Things

TWELVE YEAR-OLD ELIZABETH is no normal girl. With an imagination that makes room for mermaids and magic in everyday life, she lives every moment to the fullest. Yet her joyful world crumbles around her when two planes bring down the Twin Towers and tear her family apart. Thousands of miles away, yet still touched by this tragedy, Elizabeth is swimming in a sea of loss. She finally finds hope when she meets her kindred spirit in 8 year-old Brandt and his 13 year-old brother, Jared.

Brandt and Jared, two boys as different as Oreo and milk and just as inseparable, arrive on the island to escape the mushroom of sorrow that bloomed above their lives in the wake of the tragedy. Elizabeth shows them a new way to look at the world and they help her to laugh again. But can Elizabeth and Brandt help their families see that when life brings showers of sadness, it's okay to dance in the rain?

Set against the dazzling beauty of the Dominican Republic, *Dancing in the Rain* explores the impact of the tragic fall of the Twin Towers on two Caribbean families. It is a lyrical, well-crafted tale about finding joy in the face of loss.

Dancing in the Rain won a Burt Award for Caribbean Literature (2015) prize.